# Bittersweet Breadcrumbs

Aster Rye

Paperback ISBN: 979-8-9877140-9-6

Lily Fern Books

Cover Design: Brian Larsen

Cover photo and art: Kami Larsen

This is a work of fiction. Names, characters, places, and incidents are the products of the author's imagination or are used fictitiously and any resemblance to persons living or dead are coincidence.

For the readers—those who read what they want, when they want

# 1

RAIN poured down in icy waves, drenching the antique cobbled streets of the tiny tourist town. It was as if the heavens themselves had unleashed their tears upon the world below. The damp atmosphere matched Doria James' mood completely. As she sprinted through the storm, her wavy dark hair plastered itself to her face and her equally dark eyes narrowed against the onslaught. Her work uniform clung to her curves as she shivered. Despite what the calendar said, the winter hadn't yet given up its icy temperatures in favor of the spring warmth, and her choice of light coat was a mistake she planned never to make again. Still, she gritted her teeth and pressed on.

"Guess I'm getting soggy," she muttered under her breath as she splashed through yet another rain-filled gutter.

The events of the day had been bad enough. Now she was going to return home looking and feeling like something flushed down the toilet. Her work at the café was generally decent, but that day had been particularly awful. After dealing with the leering advances of two repulsive men who seemed to believe that good service meant she should act flattered by their crude advances, she'd also dropped a tray of pancakes and then lost a sizable tip when she'd left it on the table to run off and grab the mop bucket. For all she knew, it was the same pair of jerks who'd taken the money.

"A-holes," she hissed, pushing away the memories and focusing on getting home as quickly as possible. The rain showed no signs of relenting and even with her head down and her arms wrapped tightly around herself, she could feel the chill seeping beneath her skin and deep into her bones.

Days like this reminded her of exactly what terrible life choices could do to a person. It seemed like a lifetime ago that she'd given up on college and her dream of being a librarian in order to follow her jackass boyfriend across the country. And that had worked out *so well*. It took him all of two months to dump her and leave her stranded in the little town she now called home—a far cry from the university and city life she'd loved so much.

A handful of years after what she thought of as "the year of unending feces", she was finally getting back on her feet. She knew better than most that people could be cruel and deceitful, and the day's events had only reinforced the notion. She was tough, but beneath it all, she longed for escape from the harsh reality of life. She found said escape in her books.  Books had never betrayed her. Not once. Unless of course, you counted the plot twist you didn't see coming or the five-star read with a one star ending.

It was the stack of old paperbacks she'd scored that week at a rummage sale she thought of as she dashed through the rain. Soon enough, she'd be curled up on her sofa, a mug of steaming tea in one hand and a dog-eared novel in the other. The idea made her move her legs just a tinge faster.

The howling wind seemed to match Doria's turbulent mood as she hurried along the slick concrete walkways.  Just when she thought it couldn't get worse, a fierce gust tore through the street, nearly knocking her off her feet. Nearby, a tree branch snapped and crashed to the pavement below.

"For fuck's sake," she breathed, trying to calm her pounding heart. The branch had nearly taken her head off. Storms like this could be deadly. She needed to find somewhere to pop in for a few minutes while it passed.

Her options were limited, though. This wasn't her favorite part of town. Far from the tourist shops and quaint picturesque storefronts, she was in a firm locals-only area. She didn't fancy the idea of getting stuck in either the sleezy bar on the corner or the used appliance store. She'd been in there once, and the owner reminded her a little too much of her ex. Scanning around, she noticed something she'd never seen before. Nestled between the dry cleaners and a clothing consignment store was an old worn wooden sign which read "VESPERTINE BOOKS". Doria paused for a moment, curiosity piqued despite the rain pelting her mercilessly.

She didn't have the money for new books, but it couldn't hurt to look.

With a deep breath, Doria pushed the door open. Excitement mingled with the knowledge that she could only look—not buy. She stomped off her boots but knew she'd be dripping water everywhere, despite her best efforts. Stepping in from the street, she was met with a warm inviting sanctuary, a cocoon of knowledge and comfort. Shelves lined the walls and filled the open area with row upon row of volumes that beckoned to Doria like old friends.

A bell jingled as the door closed. "Hello?" she called out tentatively, her voice swallowed in the vast expanse of paper and ink. The whole place looked deserted.

"Welcome," a soft voice said from the corner of the shop where a pair of overstuffed chairs sat.

Doria turned, finding herself looking at a beautiful middle-aged woman lounging in one of the deep indigo chairs, a book open on her lap. She had short hair, cut into a face-framing pixie style and crystal blue eyes that seemed to know things they shouldn't.

"Let me know if you need help finding anything," she said.

Doria glanced around. She didn't see anyone else in the shop or behind the high counter that ran along the front wall. "Do you work here?"

"No," the woman replied. "But I'm pretty familiar with the place. Miles is here somewhere though. If you'd like, I can track him down."

"Uh, oh. No. Thank you," Doria replied, still taking in the wonderful surroundings. "I'll just be browsing if that's cool. The storm's getting pretty wicked out there."

"Of course," the woman nodded, a knowing look on her face. "I figured as much. Take a look around. I'm sure you'll end up finding something you can't live without."

"Thanks," Doria said, her voice barely audible. She turned away from the woman and stepped back into the first row of shelves. They seemed to stretch out far deeper than she would have imagined. From the outside, the place looked no bigger than a postage stamp, but inside, it rivaled some of the city shops she'd loved so much as a kid.

As she wandered deeper, her eyes fell on the huge selection of books. Old expensive tomes mingled with new releases and what could only be collector's editions—no more than three or four copies of even the newest books on the shelves. It was just what she needed after her horrendous day. A wonderful find. Magical even.

Doria thought of her roommate Felicity. She'd grown up in the small town and knew *everything* about *everything* interesting in town. Doria made a mental note to berate her later that night for failing to tell her best friend that this place existed. As she passed a low shelf, she grabbed a leather-bound volume of Poe short stories and poems from among the stacks. It probably cost more than she'd make in a month, even with good tips. Despite the price, she had a hard time setting it down. It brought a balm to her soul and the idea of parting with it now was unthinkable.

She wandered further along the aisle and the books seemed to get older and more rare. Her fingers brushed over delicate bindings, feeling the weight of the histories and the secrets they held.

"Looking for a little light reading?" a voice asked over her shoulder and Doria yelped. She had been certain no one was behind her as she'd studied the books, but obviously, she was wrong.

"Sorry," she stammered. "You scared the shit out of me."

A short stocky man stood staring at her, completely unabashed. His hair was a light sandy color and thinning on the top despite his apparent age being not much past thirty. "Yes well. It's unusual to find folks this far back in the stacks," he explained.

"Oh? I didn't realize. Sometimes I get a little carried away where books are concerned. They just seem to grab hold and keep me. You must be Miles?"

The man scoffed. "Hardly. My name's Peter Smith."

"Do you not work here then?"

"No indeed. I do not. I just check in on things from time to time." He studied her from the corner of his eye, his lips turned down slightly. "But I agree. There's something about old books in particular, isn't there? The words of the past can teach us valuable lessons for the present. Wouldn't you say?"

Well then… weirdo.

Not really knowing how to reply, Doria nodded and moved a step back. "Well, I'll just keep exploring then."

She looked over her shoulder as she got to the end of the row. Mr. Peter Smith was still watching her. Finally, he tipped his head in her direction and headed off away from her. Something about him filled her with a mix of curiosity and unease, but within minutes, all thought of the odd little man was erased as she finally found the section of books she was looking for.

As she stumbled into the horror fiction section of the store, the worries of the day evaporated.

The light back here was dimmer, and what was there cast eerie shadows on the shelves. Rather than making her uncomfortable, however, Doria immediately felt at home among the macabre tales. As her dark eyes scanned the wall, she saw authors who had become familiar friends over the years. Savings be damned, she saw so many books she'd been longing to add to her "to be read" pile, she just couldn't control herself. Slipping the leather tomb of Poe into her bag to free up her hands, she added several other titles to her stack. She would replace the expensive book back on its shelf before she paid for the others. Her heart swelled in anticipation of the terror and suspense that awaited her between the pages.

As she bent over to reach for another title, a low voice from behind her, startled her once again. "What a lovely day for a ghost story, huh?"

For the love of all that was holy... Was it a fucking requirement to sneak up on people in this place?

Doria snapped upright, her muscles tense, and turned to face the stranger. She wasn't accustomed to being caught off guard in such rapid succession. Her eyes narrowed as she studied him. He was tall, his hair a dark chestnut brown and neatly combed. His attire was impeccably tailored, giving him an air of sophistication, she hadn't expected in a simple bookshop. But what caught her attention the most was the twinkle of enjoyment she saw in his deep-set blue eyes. It was almost as if he was happy to have startled her.

"Uh. . . yeah," she replied hesitantly, taken aback by both his sudden appearance, and how disarming he was in general. He wasn't her typical type—too polished, a little too straight-laced—but there was no denying the fact that she found him hot beyond all reason.

Her pulse was pounding a little too hard to blame merely on being startled.

"Have you read this one?" he asked, plucking a novel from the shelf. "It's really quite. . . chilling." One side of his mouth quirked up on the last word.

"Actually, I haven't," Doria said as her eyes flicked to the book in his hand. She smiled in reply before adding, "but I've heard good things."

He took a step closer to her and rather than backing up as she'd done with Peter, her feet remained firmly planted where they were. "Maybe you should give it a try," he suggested, his voice smooth as velvet. "I'm always fascinated by what folks wander into the shop and what they pick up among these shelves."

As she took the book from him, his finger grazed the back of her hand. The touch shot an excited little thrill through her. He hadn't taken his eyes from her face.

The turn of events left her off-kilter and unsettled. She cleared her throat and broke the spell.

"By the way," he said, "I'm Miles."

"Oh! This is your shop."

He sighed quietly, "Yes. It is."

"Doria James," she replied cautiously, wondering why he seemed reluctant to admit he owned the store.

"Well, Doria James. It is a pleasure to meet a fellow book enthusiast." He leaned closer and studied the stack of books she held in her hands. "Far be it from me to judge another's taste in literature, but that's quite the stack of bloody books you've chosen."

She tilted her head to the side and pursed her lips. "What can I say, I like the darker stuff."

"Horror only?"

"No, Mr. . .?" She realized he'd only given his first name.

"Oak. But please, just call me Miles."

"Alright Miles. I love a great thriller and the occasional mystery. But not the cozy stuff. I need the edge-of-your-seat, can't-sleep-at-night, kind of book."

A divot formed between his brows. "Fascinating. Are you sure I can't interest you in something a little more. . . I don't know. Romantic? The rom-coms are just around…"

He didn't get to finish the sentence before Doria's temper flared. "What the hell makes you think I should be interested in a fucking rom-com?" she snapped. Her grip on the stack of books tightened and she was at risk of dropping the whole bunch.

"Hey. I certainly didn't mean to offend you," Miles said, raising his hands in surrender, his eyes widening at her tone. The warmth never left his voice, though, and that only served to irritate Doria further.

"Because I'm a woman? Not every girl likes to swoon over the bare-chested men and flowery meet cutes. There should be more to a story than a predictable ending and a spicy scene or two."

"I completely agree. Everyone is entitled to read what they enjoy. I didn't mean to upset you."

"Save your apologies," Doria muttered, her face heating with frustration at a ruined evening and the shame of her reaction to his words. It had been a long day. A long week. A long couple of years. But even so, she hated how snappish she was. It wasn't this guy's fault. In truth, she couldn't afford the books anyway.

With a sad little huff, she placed the stack on a nearby end table, the sound echoing through the store. "I think I'll just be on my way. You don't mind reshelving these do you?"

"Really. I'm sorry. I just know what's popular these days. You don't need to leave." He ran a hand through his dark hair and sighed even louder.

"It's . . ." Doria didn't know what to say. She had been out of sorts ever since she ducked into the shop. "I just. . . I can't. Never mind. You have a beautiful shop here. I hope you do well."

As she turned to walk back toward the door, her eyes caught on a new thriller displayed on an endcap. The blood splatter and bold red lettering on the cover called to her, making her stop long enough to pick it up and read the back cover. After mentally adding it to the growing list of books to hunt down later, she set her shoulders and kept walking.

She looked around for the beautiful pixie-haired woman, or the odd little Peter Smith, but the store appeared to be empty of anyone other than her and the shopkeeper. He'd made it to the front and Doria saw he wore a mixture of confusion and concern on his handsome face. He'd certainly riled her, but she still couldn't deny the magnetic pull she felt when looking at him. It both intrigued and terrified her.

Doria pulled her coat around her tightly, all thoughts of horror and thrillers gone as she spied the rain still coming down outside. She hunched her shoulders and had turned the knob on the front door when a firm grip closed around her wrist. She jerked back, her breath catching in her throat.

"Ms. James," Miles said, his voice low and measured. "I believe you have something that does not belong to you."

Doria had no idea what he was talking about and she would be damned if she was going to let someone man handle her, no matter how unbelievably handsome he was. She tried to pull her arm away, but his grip held firm. Her dark eyes met his blue ones, defiance battling with just the slightest trace of heat.

"Look asshole," she demanded, "I don't have any idea what you're talking about. Let. Me. Go." Despite the tough words, there was a tremor in her voice that betrayed her unease.

His mouth quirked up in a half smile. "Only," he lifted his brow, "if you give me the book you have in your bag."

Ah . . . shit. The Poe volume. She'd been so completely unnerved by the previous interaction, she'd forgotten about the damned book.

She squinched her nose up and closed her eyes. "I forgot." She opened them and looked at his skeptical face. "Really. I only meant to hold it there until I could return it to the shelf."

"I see." He released her wrist and crossed his arms over his chest.

"Oh god." She fumbled open her bag, pulled out the leather-bound beauty, and handed it to him. "I feel like an idiot. You aren't going to call the police or anything, are you?" That was the last thing Doria needed in her life right then.

"I think that would be a little extreme, don't you?"

Relief washed through her. "Yes," she said in a small voice and looked up at him.

"How about we make a deal?" Miles said. "I won't make a fuss over this if you take a book of *my* choosing home with you, read it, and return it to me in the next few days. Then we can discuss it like civilized people."

"A book of your choosing?" She studied him and visions of stuffy classics or non-fiction history texts danced through her head.

"Yes. My choosing. One I myself have enjoyed and think you might like. If, that is, you're willing to give it a chance and not judge it too harshly before you've read it."

"Really?" Doria scoffed; her brows raised skeptically. "Why?"

"Because Ms. James," he said, his cool eyes locking with hers, "I have a feeling you might actually enjoy it more than you think."

Doria hesitated, weighing her options. She didn't really think he'd call the police, and even if he did, she could easily explain the mix-up. But she was tired and didn't want the hassle of sticking around to find out. Plus, she couldn't easily deny her curiosity about what sort of mystery book Miles might want her to read.

"Fine," she relented at last, her voice barely above a whisper. "Let's see the damn book then."

Miles guided her to the fantasy romance section, a small smile playing on his lips.

Doria groaned when she saw the selection in front of her. Not just fantasy. But fantasy *romance*. His choice could not possibly get any worse.

Miles scanned the shelves before selecting a thin hardcover with gilded detail on the jacket. Doria rolled her eyes at the collection of short stories he extended to her. She was half tempted to throw the book at him and head for the door.

"Give it a chance," he urged, his voice soft. "Who knows? You might find something in these pages that speaks to you."

Doria hesitated. Her pride and the tough face she showed to the world were warring with her curiosity. Finally, she sighed and tucked the book into her satchel to keep it safe from the rain. "Fine. But I want you to be aware, when I despise it, I'm going to let you know."

He extended his hand. "Fair enough. And to make it a bit easier, I only ask that you read one of the stories in there. You don't have to finish the whole thing."

She cocked her head but shook his hand. "I should be able to stomach one short story. I'll bring your book back tomorrow when I get off."

He grinned. "I'll be anxiously awaiting your arrival."

# 2

THE rain was letting up as she hurried to the tiny apartment she shared with Felicity. Something about the deal she'd made with the enigmatic man in the shop left her feeling off balance. She couldn't quite discern his motives, and if there was one thing Doria knew, it was that everyone had a motive.

Whatever his reasons were, she didn't plan on backing out of the deal. One story wouldn't kill her and she was actually kind of excited about returning to tell him exactly how much she hated the book. Because she *was* going to hate it. Even as a kid, she'd never gone in for all the fluffy-frilly-feel-good stuff. The tales of sleeping princesses awakened by true love's kiss and happily-ever-after were just fairy tales, nothing more. If she hadn't believed it as a fresh faced and innocent child, she certainly did not as a jaded and cynical adult.

By the time she trudged up the steps to her apartment, her clothes were once again sodden and clung to her like a second skin. Shivering, she locked the door behind her and toed off her boots as she sat the satchel on the ground. All the damp clothing got tossed in a pile before she slipped into her most comfortable pajama pants and a dry tank top, immediately feeling better.

The evening called for a hot bowl of soup, so Doria dumped a can into a microwave-safe bowl and popped it in to warm, then retrieved the book from her bag. She studied the cover. A misty forest sparkled with shimmering lights under the gold embossed title. Definitely not her go-to cover aesthetic, but a deal was a deal. When the microwave dinged, she carried the bowl with her to the couch and took a cautious sip. "All right then, let's give this a go."

Within moments of cracking the spine, she was in her happy place. Ink and paper. The weight and feel of the book in her hands. The anticipation of drifting away to another world as she lost herself in the plot.

Within a few moments, however, she regretted making the deal with Miles. The prose was so light and airy, she felt like she could float it on a bubble.

Doria grimaced and wondered if being arrested would have been less painful than enduring this literary torment.

Refusing to give up just yet, she flipped through the book to the second story and began to read.

## Bastian and Adela

*It was too fucking cold to be out in the woods. Adela could barely feel her hands, chapped and frozen as they were.*

Well at least this one started out with an F-bomb. There was hope for it yet. She sipped her soup and made herself focus. She started again.

## Bastian and Adela

*It was too fucking cold to be out in the woods. Adela could barely feel her hands, chapped and frozen as they were. She'd made sure to grab her thickest gloves and her fur-trimmed cloak when Bastian showed up just after moonrise, but despite the coins she spent on them, the wind bit through the wool as if it were a thin cotton shift.*

*She was sure Bastian could hear her teeth chattering, but there was no chance she would complain and have him suggest she return to the warmth of her cottage and the crackling embers she'd left there in the hearth. It had taken months of prodding to get him to allow her to accompany him on a night patrol. Those months had been awkward enough, thanks to her own foolishness. She would be damned if she was going to give up just because her nose was numb.*

*If the cold bothered him as well, she couldn't see it. Bastian stood tall and straight, every move fluid and confident. She smiled to herself when she thought of the thin lanky child he'd been when they first met. Too shy to speak to her, much less lead a group of hunters, tracking the most dangerous of prey without even a torchlight to guide them.*

*"This way." He pointed to a break in the foliage surrounding them. Under the silvery moonlight, Adela could just make out the dark smudges on the leaves. Did the witch bleed black blood or was it only a trick of the shadows?*

*Bastian tore a bit of white cloth and tied it to a low hanging branch above the worn footpath, took two long strides, then held the thick branches back to allow her passage through the underbrush. It was the fifth strip of cloth he'd used in the last hour. Adela thought of her father's warning when she was a child. The woods are tricky. Never go in alone.*

*"Are you certain it's her blood?" She asked, just to take her mind off what else might be lurking along the paths.*

*"Nothing is certain in these woods Adela. But, I'm as close to convinced as I can be. Nicol claims to have hit her with his arrow, and his word is as good as his bow. If he says he hit her, he did."*

*"She's moving fairly swiftly for a woman so wounded," Adela said.*

*"True, but she's no typical woman. Remember that, Adela. No matter what you see, no matter what you hear.*

*When we catch her, remember that. She is no typical woman. She'll rip your heart from your chest and eat it if she can."*

*He put a hand out and signaled Adela to stop. Then he drew his finger to his lips. Enough talk.*

*Adela's eyes grew wide and she nodded. They must be close if Bastian was silencing her.*

*They came to a small stream crusted with ice along the rock and pebble banks. Adela followed Bastian across, keeping to the stones that poked above the surface. The last thing either of them needed was to have sodden boots. It would only speed up the frostbite.*

*They continued on in silence for several more minutes. The pair rounded a large oak and Bastian swore. "Damn these woods and the harpy who calls them home."*

*In the pale light of the stars, Adela didn't immediately understand what had caused the reaction. Then she saw it. Fluttering just above her sightline, tied neatly to a dangling branch, was a clean white strip of cloth. One of the markers Bastian had left to help them find their way home again.*

*"Oh," she said, voice small.*

*"Oh indeed, Adela. I fear I may have led you astray."*

*"No matter," she responded, pushing more confidence into her voice than she felt. "We'll pick up the trail and continue onward."*

*"Do you think I've not noticed the chattering and shivering? I can't keep you out in these conditions. It's time to head home."*

*"I'm fine," she bit out.*

*"I don't think you are."*

*Adela glared at Bastian. "Don't you dare try to tell me how I feel, Bastian."*

*He raised his hands in surrender. "Sorry. I didn't mean any harm. It's just. . . you aren't accustomed to the conditions of the forest. Hell, it's even miserable for me."*

*Adela used the back of one gloved hand and wiped at her nose. The cold lashed at her cheeks and she felt it sting as the water in her eyes turned to icy crystals in her lashes.*

*"You've been amazing. All night. But it's cold and I'm afraid our quarry has gotten the better of us once again," he said, his voice tired and worn.*

*Adela wondered how many more nights Bastian would be forced from his bed to hunt the wretched woman. He'd been unsuccessful for months. Given that he and the other hunters could only go out on clear nights, or risk the witch seeing them with their torches and lamps, the chances were limited. It made Adela sick that she now hoped for overcast evenings, knowing the clouds would keep Bastian home safe in his bed. Or as safe as any of them were.*

*In the last six moon cycles, just as many villagers had gone missing. The witch seemed to have no preference for her prey. Young men and village maidens, a new widow, and a dashing captain of the guard. Each had been taken. Despite barred doors and closed windows, the witch was able to lure them away in the dead of night, never to be seen again.*

*"All right." Adela managed a weak smile. "My bed does sound fairly splendid right about now."*

*"It does indeed," Bastian replied. Then realizing what he'd said, he cleared his throat. "I mean, my bed does as well."*

*Adela smiled to herself. Perhaps Bastian was starting to feel the same pull toward her that she'd been experiencing toward him for the last year or so.*

*"We should keep moving," he said into the silence.*

*Adela pulled her cloak tighter around herself and watched as he reached up and slit the white cloth free of the branch before stuffing it into his pack. They came upon two more cloth strips before the markers seemed to disappear from the path completely.*

"It was here," Bastian hissed. "I know it was here. This branch. Next to the oak with the toadstools at the base."

Adela nodded and stared into the dark. She was sure this had been the spot of his first marker as well. Perhaps the wind had taken it. Or a bird needing fodder for its nest.

"I think we should camp," she said. "Before we get even further turned around. If one of the others comes by, we'll hear and yell them down." The idea of spending the night in the woods was not one she savored but becoming further lost sounded worse.

"We can build a small fire," he agreed. "The risk is likely passed."

Bastian hunted around for a few logs as Adela collected up what kindling she could. They agreed on a dry flat space near the large oak and Bastian cleared an area in the loamy soil where they could build their fire. Bastian handed his flint box to Adela and she made quick work of getting the flames going.

Bastian took one last walk around the area, searching for threats hidden in the dark and shadows, then settled down beside Adela where she crouched by the flames.

"You should try to sleep," he told her.

"Not just yet," she replied. "I'm too jittery at the moment."

Holding her hands up to the flames, Adela willed the circulation to return to her icy fingers. Bastian tossed a large log on the kindling, sending embers up into the surrounding dark.

They sat in silence and stared into the flames.

"Lay this out and then you can cover yourself with your cloak." Bastian handed her a rough woolen blanket he'd pulled from his pack. "It's not much, but it'll help."

"And what about you?"

"I'll be fine," he said as he stood and walked to the other side of the fire.

*"Oh, for fuck's sake, Bastian. I promise not to touch you." The words were sharp, but Adela couldn't help it. Ever since the night eight months ago, when she'd had one too many ciders and had tried to kiss him, Bastian had been different. Gone was her constant companion and best friend, and in his place was this brooding man she hardly recognized.*

*"Quite the mouth you've got on you these days," he growled back.*

*"I'm just tired of it." She crossed her hands over her chest.*

*"Tired of what, exactly?"*

*"Tired of you keeping me at a constant arm's length. It was a mistake. I was drunk. I don't know how many times I need to apologize," she insisted.*

*"And I don't know how many times I need to tell you, no apology is needed." The firelight danced in his brown eyes and Adela could see the cold turn his breath to fog as he released a long exhale.*

*"Just come sit back down." She softened her voice. Arguing wasn't going to do them any good.*

*"Only if you try to sleep," he replied.*

*"Fine."*

*Adela stretched out along the blanket and did as he suggested, pulling her cloak over herself. Once again, she thanked the stars for her thick leather leggings and down-lined vest. She felt Bastian lay down next to her, his familiar form a comfort to her. Despite her earlier protests, she felt her eyes grow heavy almost immediately. Within minutes, the mixture of wood smoke, the feel of Bastian beside her, and the murmuring of the wind through the trees had her drifting off.*

*Some hours later, Adela surfaced from sleep to feel Bastian stretched out behind her. He'd apparently gotten tired of the cold and had burrowed under the fur of her cloak* to sleep. The light had changed and she could sense dawn approaching. The fire had died down, but the coals still radiated a bit of heat. She snuggled back on instinct. He groaned quietly at the movement and Adela was surprised to feel the hard length of him against her as her body encountered his.

Her eyes popped open as she realized what was happening.

"Don't move," he rasped against her neck. "Just. . . don't move."

"I thought..." she began.

"Doesn't matter what you thought. Right now, I want you right where you are."

There was a strange fluttering in her chest and an ache from her breasts to her thighs. She exhaled and pushed back further into him. He groaned louder.

Bastian wrapped an arm over her side and across her chest, cupping her breast through the layers of fabric. Now it was her turn to moan.

Bastian nuzzled her neck from behind and pushed her tangled mass of chestnut hair away from her ear before grabbing her earlobe and sucking it gently into his mouth. He bit down lightly, then trailed a line of kisses down her neck. Adela turned her face to his and Bastian immediately captured her mouth.

She couldn't think. She only knew she had wanted this for so long. And now? Now she was pushing all that want into this kiss. As she opened her mouth to him, he groaned and pulled his arms tighter around her.

Her back still to him, Adela's breath grew ragged as she lost herself in the kiss. She wanted to wrap her arms around him and draw him closer. Breaking the connection, she pulled back in an effort to reposition herself.

"I told you not to move." His voice was low and ragged. His eyes full of need.

*She rolled to her back and pulled him toward her. "Since when have I ever listened to you?"*

*"Since never." He rolled over her, supporting his weight on his forearms as his hand dove into her hair. Then he was devouring her mouth once again.*

*If Adela had been grateful for her leather leggings before, she was doubly so now. A skirt would have tangled and restricted her, but the pants gave her the freedom to move, allowing his knee to part her legs.*

*The sound he made when she moved against him was delicious.*

*The sound that followed, was not.*

*Just as she thought she'd die of wanting, a scream tore through the early morning air.*

*Bastian flinched.*

*"What was that?" she whispered.*

*"I'm not sure."*

*The scream split the air a second time and Bastian was up and moving. He kicked dirt over the last embers of the fire and scooped up his pack. Adela was right behind him. All thoughts of the bliss she'd just experienced gone in a heartbeat. She fastened her cloak as he shoved the blanket into his pack and headed off in the direction of the screams.*

"Seriously?" Doria grumbled, disdain thick in the air. "This is what he thought I'd like. Fuck me."

Despite her mounting frustration, she had no desire to start yet another story from the book, so she elected to trudge on. Taking another gulp of the now lukewarm soup, she skimmed through the last page, looking for where she'd left off, hoping against all reason that the story might improve.

"*Maybe it was just a bird,*" Adela panted as she caught up to Bastian.

"*Maybe.*" His tone was doubtful.

The two had been running through the woods for over an hour, chasing the occasional shriek. In her heart, Adela knew it was no bird. The screams were all too human. But what could cause a person to make that noise?

"*What do we do now?*" she asked.

Bastian turned to her and sighed. "*I don't know. Part of me wants nothing more than to get you home. But as appealing as that sounds, I could never live with myself if we didn't do what we could to help, or at least see. . .*"

He didn't need to finish. Adela knew they might already be too late. No one knew what the witch did with those she took, but there were stories. Torture. Death. Servitude. She'd recently even heard the schoolchildren telling one another that the witch had a taste for human flesh. How the stories came to be, she didn't know or care. The idea sent a shiver down her spine.

They walked on.

As the sun began to climb higher into the sky, hunger began to claw at Adela. And with the hunger came a sense of foreboding. Neither of them had planned to be out this long and they hadn't packed any provisions.

The trees took on a sinister feel and Adela became certain that they were walking around in circles. Each turn took them to another that seemed both foreign and familiar.

Her head was swimming. One moment she was on the path with Bastian and then next she was lost in her memories. Adela as a scrawny slip of a girl. Her mother, dead in her grave. Not four months later, Adela's father announcing he was to marry. Her stepmother, a brutal woman. Adela, escaping the house and another beating one morning. Finding Bastian playing by the river. Knowing him from the schoolyard but never having spoken to him. Him so shy. So *quiet. They'd become inseparable. His father, also good with his fists. Growing up, side by side. Always there for one another. The hurt look in his eyes when, at sixteen, she'd agreed to go to the spring festival with Hans. The angry look in his eyes when she'd told him what Hans had done to her after the festival. The calm look in his eyes years later when Hans had had an accident near the river and had been found downstream, head caved in. Bastian, as he'd become in recent years. Tall, broad, and handsome. All the village girls chasing after him. Still quiet, but now in a confident way. Adela, still his friend, but now also one of the women who wished he'd look at her like a woman and not just as his childhood friend.*

*Lost as she was in her thoughts, Adela didn't see Bastian stop on the path and ran smack into his back.*

*"Sorry," she mumbled, then peered over his shoulder to see what it was that had caused him to pause.*

*The path they were on opened into a wide green clearing. A stream ran through one side and a small vegetable patch was on the other. Set back from the path, nestled against the far side of the trees, stood a pristine stone cottage. The windows were open and smoke rose from the chimney in lackadaisical loops. From the windows, faint music could be heard, and the smell of warm bread drifted out to meet them.*

*Adela's mouth watered at the scent.*

*"Come on Bastian. Perhaps whoever owns this place can point us in the right direction. A slice of bread wouldn't be turned down either." Adela moved to go around him but was stopped by a firm hand on her arm.*

*"Remember what I said. She is no ordinary woman."*

*Adela scoffed. "Surely you can't think the witch lives here."*

"I can and I do." He jerked his head toward the side of the cottage where Adela had noted the vegetable garden and her heart skipped a beat.

Between the stone wall of the structure and the garden itself stood a series of statues. Six statues to be exact. All six beautiful nudes in graceful poses. All six with familiar faces. All six missing from their village.

"How can...how are they..." Adela couldn't decide how to voice what she was thinking. Were these the villagers turned to stone, or simply amazing likenesses? And if simply likenesses, how had they been done with such accuracy? More importantly, where were the villagers themselves?

As she stood there staring, the door from the cottage opened and Bastian pulled Adela to the side, hiding them behind a large bank of shrubs.

Exiting the building was a beautiful woman. She had long golden hair worn loose down her back and, despite the cold, was clad in only a thin silk shift the color of the sky just after sunset. The material clung to her curves and left her arms exposed. She wore no shoes and seemed unhampered by the bite of frost in the air.

Humming to herself, she turned in the doorway and pulled another marble statue from the building. Grabbing it below the arms, she tipped it towards herself and drug it through the grass to join the others. Given its life-sized proportions, the stone must have been immensely heavy, Adela thought. And yet, the woman acted as though it weighed nothing at all.

From where she hid, Adela thought the statues looked to be made of pale grey marble but couldn't be certain.

As the witch– for surely this must be her– straightened the newest addition to her collection, Bastian swore softly. The statue was as lovely as the others–strong arms raised to draw back the bow in his hands, hips cocked slightly, lean *waist and thighs. And the face. The face was that of Nicol. Good with a bow, but apparently not good enough.*

*Had those been Nicol's screams they followed to this place? Adela couldn't be certain, but she thought the answer was likely yes.*

*Adela was pulled from her thoughts by a sweet, high voice. "You can come out from there, dear ones. No sense in hiding. I know you're there. Come see my collection for yourselves."*

*The witch turned and stared directly at them, as if she could see them perfectly. Adela wanted to run, but knew she wouldn't. The people, the villagers. They needed help. If they could, in fact, be helped.  But how? Bastian took her gloved hand in his and squeezed. Then as one, they stood and faced the lovely monster.*

*"I do so love beautiful things," the witch said with a smile.*

*The witch waited for them as they crossed the yard to where she stood among the lifelike statues. Each likeness was done to the smallest detail. Individual hairs could be seen, the outlines of muscles defined, a beauty mark positioned just so. Even the small scar Nicol had below his left eye was visible in the finest detail. Only the eyes were wrong, Adela noted. No pupils or irises, just blank flat orbs. Despite this, Adela was convinced these weren't simply an artist's renderings, these were the villagers. How the witch had done it, she couldn't fathom.*

*The witch studied Bastian and Adela as they walked toward her and Adela felt a shiver go down her spine. Her smile widened as they stopped a few feet away, then she turned and drug her hand down the statue of Nicol. Her fingers drifted from his collarbone, over his pecs and abdomen, before stopping and resting on his naked hip.*

*"He is lovely, isn't he?" She cooed.*

*"What have you done?" Bastian demanded.*

"Nothing he didn't deserve after shooting me with that vile arrow of his," the witch responded. "Lucky for me, he gave chase. How could he have known I heal a bit quicker than most?"

"Is he even alive?" Adela asked. "You have to undo this."

"Alive or dead. What difference does it make? He's not going anywhere, and it won't be undone. Like I said, I enjoy beautiful things. Now come along."

She snapped her fingers and Adela felt her muscles tighten. Every bit of her self-control was gone and no matter how hard she struggled, she was helpless. Her body moved of its own volition, following first the witch and then Bastian into the open door of the cottage. Once she was over the threshold, the door snapped shut behind her.

Like the exterior of the cottage, the interior was not at all what Adela felt a witch's lair should be. It was bright and airy. Simple, but elegantly furnished with sturdy wood and velvet. A thick rug covered the cold stone floor. Sunlight streamed through the open windows and there was, in fact, a hot loaf of bread cooling on the table.

"Sit," the witch demanded without turning around. Adela and Bastian's bodies did as they were told, settling in next to one another on a low wooden bench. Adela inhaled Bastian's scent— wood smoke and cedar. If her fate was to be a statue in this woman's garden, she wanted to keep the scent of him with her for as long as she could.

The witch moved closer to her hearth and used a long pole to stoke the coals glowing within it. "I don't know how you managed to find this place, but I'm ever so happy you did. It's a shame the fires have spent their magic. It'll be three days more before I can make use of them again. I suppose I'll just have to savor the anticipation."

"What do you mean?" Bastian asked.

*"You don't think the figures out there made themselves, do you?" She turned back to them, and Adela marveled at the woman's seduction. Her skin was like porcelain and her eyes like cool depthless pools. High cheekbones and full lips. Where the silk pulled taut against her breasts, little was left to the imagination. She might just as well have been naked like her collection. She was the very epitome of beauty. But under the surface, Adela sensed the roiling mass of ugliness at her core. "The fire is the key and it takes time to regenerate. My pet with the bow has used all of its magic. So now I must wait."*

*She walked over and placed a hand on Adela's cheek, a hunger growing in the depths of her beautiful eyes. "Or more accurately, we wait."*

*Adela tried to pull back from the woman's touch, but her body was still not her own. She was trapped where she sat.*

*"Get your hands off of her," Bastian growled. The witch only chuckled.*

*"Please," he said then. "Please. Let Adela go and I'll stay willingly. You can add me to your garden. Just let her go."*

*If he honestly thought Adela would walk out of there without him, he was insane. She'd rather die than leave him to such a cruel fate.*

*It didn't matter either way. The witch had no intention of letting either of them leave.*

*"Such the hero. But I'm afraid it won't do. I've already got it all planned out. I knew the moment I sensed you lurking there. The limbs entwined, the lips touching. I'll call you 'The Lover's Embrace'. The fire will need a recharge after, but with such a boon as this, I can afford to be patient."*

*A taste for human flesh indeed.*

Huh? Doria thought. Maybe the witch will change her mind and eat them instead. The tale could have a happy ending after all. Or at the very least, one Doria would appreciate.

# 3

It was getting late and Doria had to work the next day, but she wanted to power through and finish the story. Felicity wasn't home yet anyway, and she would certainly enjoy hearing about the Doria's crazy day.

She kept reading.

*Three days. Adela and Bastian had three days to come up with a plan for escape. Three days before the witch used her magic to lock them in an eternal embrace and place them in her garden. Three days for Adela to think about the loss of her future with the man she'd loved nearly her entire life. Three days—unless she could come up with a plan.*

*"Now it's been a long night, and I need my beauty rest," the witch giggled before continuing. "But I can't very well leave the two of you perched like that, now, can I? What sort of host would I be then? I'm not used to housing guests, you know."*

*She stepped back and placed a finger on her chin. "I've got just the thing!" She turned and snapped again,* sending Adela and Bastian to their feet and following in her wake. "It's not much, but it will simply have to do."

The witch opened a door on the far side of the hearth. It looked to be a storage cupboard of some sort. Shelves lined one wall, but they were mostly bare, save for a handful of potatoes, some carrots, a block of hard cheese, and a basket of small apples. In the corner stood a broom and a wash pale.

The witch grabbed the broom and placed it outside of the cupboard. "Can't have you getting any bright ideas, now can we?"

She turned to look at them. Bastian's face was hard as he stared back, but Adela managed a weak smile. "We can rest in there?"

"Of course, dear one. I need you looking your best when the time comes. I'm even going to go so far as to remove the enchantment I have on you." She smiled brightly. "But," she held up a finger, "I'll need to lock the door. Who knows what you'd get up to if I let you wander about the place. And," now she held out her hand, "I need those filthy rags. You both stink to no end."

The smile slipped from Adela's face as she stared blankly at the witch. "I don't understand."

"Your clothes," the witch snapped. "Give me your clothes."

Bastian's lips thinned to a harsh line. He gave a brief shake of his head. "No."

"It's not a request." When he didn't move, the witch drew nearer. "I said. Give. Me. Your. Clothes." She snapped her fingers and Bastian's body grew rigid. The strain on his face evident as his hands moved to the clasps on his jacket.

"You too," she said to Adela.

There was no need for the witch to enchant her. Adela didn't fight. She unclasped her cloak and unlaced her leather *leggings. Toeing off her boots, she tried not to look at Bastian.*

*The witch, however, drank him in with her eyes. His face grew red as he pulled the shirt over his shoulders and dropped his leather breeches in a puddle on the ground. Adela pulled off her own down vest and the shirt beneath it. Then she slid the off the leggings and added them to the pile.*

*"Here you are, dear one. For not fighting." The witch handed Adela a soft homespun blanket. "Use that to cover yourself if you like." She tilted her head toward the cupboard.*

*Adela took the offering and wrapped it around her body, then stepped into the small space. Bastian stumbled in after her, putting his hands up to catch himself against the back wall. The door clicked shut behind them and Adela sank onto the ground in the near total darkness.*

Of course. Now they're naked and in a closet. Could it be any more cliché? Doria really hoped the witch would eat them. It had better be good and gory. Lots of screaming.

*"Here," she said, and offered an edge of the blanket to Bastian. "It's no use resisting her."*

*"You're giving up that easily?"*

*"No. I am choosing my battles Bastion." She grabbed his hand and pulled him down next to her. A faint sliver of light shone under the crack in the door. It was just enough to make out the vague outline of Bastian. She spread the blanket across his lap, careful where she was touching. In a hushed whisper, she explained, "We can't fight the enchantment. That seems pretty obvious. So we need to attack this another way. We've got three days to figure a way to outsmart her."*

*The witch clambered around the small cottage for several long minutes, banging pots and singing to herself. After what felt like an eternity, the noises stopped and soon the soft sound of snoring could be heard through the door.*

*"You're right. Sorry. It's just. . . I got you into this mess and I feel like I might not be able to get you out of it."*

*"I'm the one who's been begging you to let me come along, remember?"*

*Bastian sighed, "I do remember. And this is what I get for saying yes."*

*"Trapped in a confined space. Naked. With me." She chuffed a laugh. "It's your worst nightmare come true.*

*"Hardly." He reached his arm behind her shoulders and pulled her close to his side.*

*Adela couldn't help it. Tears began to flow from her eyes and a small sob escaped.*

*"Hey. It's going to be all right. We'll figure out a way out of this. I promise," Bastian said and squeezed her tighter.*

*"I know. We have to. It's just, after this morning, I finally thought maybe things between us were going to be... I don't know..." She paused.*

*"You thought?" he prompted.*

*Adela dug the heels of her hands into her eyes. "Maybe you finally thought about me. . . like I think about you."*

*"Adela. I have always thought about you. I have always* wanted *you."*

*"But the last few months– you have done nothing but avoid me and push me away."*

*"Because you kept apologizing. Like it was something you would have only done because you were drunk." Bastian's voice was full of fire.*

*"No. I...," Adela sighed. "I just thought you didn't want me like that and I was scared I'd ruined things."*

*"Like I said. I have always wanted you, and this morning I just finally let myself give in to the wanting."*

*"Really?" Adele questioned with hope in her voice.*

*"Really," Bastian confirmed with a smile.*

*Adela didn't care that they were locked in a witch's cupboard or that they might be dead in three days' time. She didn't care that she was hungry and ashamed. She didn't care that she was dirty and needed a good bath. All she cared about was that Bastian was here with her and that he wanted her. They would figure the rest out. They would escape.*

*She let the blanket fall from where she clutched it around her breasts as she turned and took his face in the darkness. Adela kissed Bastion then. Fiercely and passionately. They may not have a lifetime ahead of them together, but they had that moment and she was going to take it.*

*After a time, he pulled away and laughed. "Of all the times I've thought about getting you naked, never in my wildest nightmares was it in circumstances like this." He kissed her again. Gently this time. "I feel like this is wrong. Having you here, in this place, like this. It's not right."*

*Adela nodded. "I understand. Just kiss me again. Nothing more. Just a kiss."*

*Bastian did as she asked. Gentle again at first, but then she moaned and he couldn't control himself. He parted her lips with his tongue and feasted on her mouth. She was panting and achy by the time they parted.*

*"We really should rest," he finally said. "We have planning to do."*

*Bastian wrapped Adela in his strong arms and held her against his chest. She tried to ignore the heat between them, but the aching in her breasts and belly was far more than she'd ever experienced. And now she wasn't sure she'd ever get to have Bastian the way her body demanded.*

Bastian seemed to sense her thoughts. "We will have time together, Adela. Rest."

She settled her head against his chest and tried to steady her breathing. She didn't sleep, but she did relax. And she plotted.

Eventually, she had a reasonable plan formulated and when she realized Bastian wasn't sleeping either, she began to tell him her idea. He mumbled back to her and together they solidified the plan.

When the witch came to open the cupboard hours later, shoving simple cotton garments at them, Adela and Bastian weren't rested, but they were prepared.

One day left. Adela had done all that she could to keep their plans hidden from the witch. If the harpy had her way, Adela and Bastian would be going in the oven to be locked in an eternal embrace the following day. Neither Adela nor Bastian had any intention of letting that happen.

Rather than fight, Adela had fallen into a pattern of doing exactly as the witch asked. She tended the garden and baked the bread. She swept up the cottage and hung the laundry. Her reward each evening was to be locked back in the cupboard with Bastian.

The witch, wanting them healthy in appearance for the day of the transformation, kept them fed and clean. It didn't matter that Adela was the one to cook and draw the buckets of warm water for the bath.

On the second morning of their captivity, Adela stepped out of the bath and donned the simple cotton shift the witch had given her the day before. Hair dripping and skin flushed, she set about the task of cutting the vegetables the witch had given her.

"I dare say, my dear, you look good enough to eat." The witch stared at her and licked her lips. "Would you not agree?" she asked Bastion with a gleam in her eye.

*Color flooded his face and he turned his head back to his own task of tending the fire.*

*Clad in loose-fitting cotton pants, Adela had a hard time keeping her eyes off him. She liked watching the muscles in his back work as he pulled and pushed at the coals. They'd been dancing around one another the past two days, not wanting to give the witch leverage over them of any kind. What would she do if she knew that Adela would do anything to spare Bastian? Instead, they kept up the charade. It was a game of sorts. Bastian trying to convince the witch he still meant to escape and Adela putting on a docile act of acceptance.*

*"Oh, my dear ones! Tomorrow is fast approaching! Can you taste the anticipation?" The witch danced around the cottage barefoot and wild. Her silk shift was a deep ruby red today and every now and then a matching hue flared in her eyes.*

*"Now, as much as I know it will pain you to hear, I have an errand to run. I've thought perhaps I should bring you along, but where I'm going, I'll need my wits. Can't have the two of you distracting me." She looked from one to the other. "So, in the cupboard with you."*

*She pointed and Bastian's body went rigid, still fighting the compulsion. Adela nodded and walked to the door of her own free will. Just as the witch was about to shut the door, Adela smiled and asked, "Would it be too much for us to be locked within the cottage itself? I've still more laundry to attend and Bastian noticed the legs on the table need to be tightened."*

*The witch paused, head cocked and eyes fierce.*

*Adela continued urgently, "If you are gone for a long spell, we might not be well rested for tomorrow."*

*The witch cocked her head. "You wouldn't be trying to trick me, dear one?"*

"Of course not. Even if I did, you surely could not be bested by a simple woman like me."

"True." The witch placed a finger to her chin. "I'll be enchanting the doors and all of the windows. Escape would be unwise and likely very. . . painful."

Adela and Bastian watched as the witch stepped over the cottage threshold, still dressed in only the silk shift and nothing more. Adela hoped she'd freeze to death in the icy air.

"I'm off to fetch the sacred wood needed for tomorrow's fire. It's a tricky task and may take some time. Be sure your tasks are completed by the time I return or things will not be the least bit pleasant for you."

She snapped her fingers and the door shut behind her, leaving Adela and Bastian alone at last.

Bastian crossed the space between them before the door had fully shut. Adela buried her face in his chest and let out a long and shaky breath. He held her close and ran his hands over her hair.

"I feel as if it's another trap," Adela said at last. "I never thought she'd actually agree."

"You can be very persuasive," he replied and kissed the top of her head.

Adela chuffed a laugh against his chest. They stood there a long minute. Neither wanting to break the connection, as if holding one another would somehow keep them safe from things to come.

Finally, Adela, voice still muffled by the wall of his chest, asked, "Where do you think she came from? The witch. She couldn't have always been here."

"No. You're right. There would have been signs. There'd be more statues. I'm certain she just arrived in these woods when the first villagers went missing. Where she came from? I can't say. Hell, perhaps?"

"Then," Adela said, "that's where we will send her back to."

*"You're so sure it'll work?" Bastian asked.*

*Adela thought for a moment before answering. "It has to, right?"*

*"It does."*

*Neither knew when their opportunity would come. Sooner would be better than later.*

*She took a shuddering breath. "If things go badly, I want you to know…"*

*He tilted her head back and cut her words off with his kiss. "Whatever it is you think I need to hear, save it for when we walk out that door."*

*She nodded and then rose to her tiptoes and placed her lips on his neck. If she couldn't tell him with words, she would tell him with her body. She kissed down the column of his throat, to the notch over his sternum. She trailed her tongue along his collarbone and he shivered. Walking around his large frame, she kissed his shoulder and then down his back, finally completing the circuit to trail her lips down his abdomen to the waist of his trousers.*

*Despite the loose fit, she could see the effect she was having on him and only hesitated a beat before rubbing her palm down the hard length of him.*

*"Adela." His voice was a throaty growl.*

*"We may never have this chance again," she said.*

*"Are you sure?" He stared at her wide eyes, the back of his knuckles rubbing over the tip of her breast.*

*She closed her eyes and reveled in the sensation. "Mmm-hmm. I'm sure."*

*Bastian captured her lips and she opened to him with hunger and longing. His hands were everywhere— in her hair, on her neck, caressing her arms and breasts. Finally, when neither could stand it a moment longer, he reached down and pulled the shift over her head.*

*His eyes grew dark. "You are the most beautiful creature I've ever seen."*

*He lifted her and Adela wrapped her legs around his waist as he walked her backward to the table.*

*When Bastian placed her on the edge and removed his trousers, Adela knew this was right. Even in this horrible place, being with Bastian was completely right.*

*The windows threw bright shafts of morning light across the table. They made love there, in the warm beams of the morning sun. It was feverish and frenzied. Adela would have liked for them to take their time, but time was one thing they did not have.*

*She knew this couldn't be the end for them. They had to survive the coming day.*

Please, please, please. Don't survive the coming day!

Doria took another sip of soup and almost gagged. It had congealed to a gelatinous sludge. She didn't realize she'd been reading for quite as long as she had been. She thumbed forward to see how many pages she had left before the story's end. Just a couple. She could do this.

*When the witch returned in the early hours of the evening, the cottage was pristine, the table had been mended and a warm dinner waited upon it. Adela still had a broom in her hand and Bastian was scrubbing the last of the pots used to make their stew.*

*The witch carried a burden of logs that seemed as if they weighed more than she did. Adela, seeing the load and still playing her part, stepped forward in an effort to assist her.*

*"Stay back, dear one," the witch commanded. "These logs aren't anything I can't handle."*

*She made it to the hearth and deposited her load with a grunt.*

*Adela had never seen logs like these. Pale olive bark coated wood the color of blood. The bark was curled and dry– skin peeling from bloodied flesh.*

*"How. . ." Adela cleared her throat. "How does it work?"*

*The witch gave a sly smile. "A lady must never reveal her secrets."*

*"Will it hurt?" The echoes of Nicol's screams still resonated in her head.*

*"Only if you fight." The witch looked pointedly at Bastian. He bared his teeth in response. The witch stared at him for a moment, then threw her head back and laughed until she was breathless. When she finally regained herself, she wiped a tear from her eye and sat at the table to eat.*

*Adela stood near the table, waiting to fetch anything the witch might need. Bastian, having finished the pots, took the broom from Adela and moved to sweep up around the oven's stone front.*

*"Did you clean the interior of the hearth as I asked?" The witch directed the question to both of them, but it was Adela who answered. "As well as we could. The door's hinge is rusty and we couldn't get it open far enough for Bastian to reach the back."*

*The witch hopped up and ran to the oven. "What do you play at? It's never been rusty before."*

*"Do be careful," Adela said. "It's still quite hot. We've been chilled and Bastian rebuilt the fire after dinner was finished."*

*The witch was outraged. "It must be clean for the enchantment to take hold."*

*"I didn't know," Adela made her voice small.*

*The witch opened the door and swung it as wide as it would go. Thankfully, the metal spoon Bastian had wedged in the hinge wasn't visible from where she knelt.*

*"Perhaps if we build up the fire, it will scour the stones clean. In the morning I can wiggle in and sweep out the ash." Adela had come to stand next to the witch as she studied the hearth.*

*"Yes. That might work. You," she pointed at Bastian, "hand me more logs."*

*Bastian did as he was told and handed the witch two of the plain pine logs from the stack. If the witch noticed that Bastian did not fight her, she didn't let on. As she called for more, he continued to hand them to her one at a time. When he switched from the pine logs to the blood-colored ones, she was so focused on the flames, she didn't notice. It was only once the flames turned grey and lavender that she startled and began to turn to look at him.*

*Adela wasted no time. Before the witch could move from her hands and knees at the opening, Adela drove her weight into the back of the harpy. The witch tumbled into the mouth of the open oven and began to shriek. Bastian, with the help from the broom, managed to push her deeper into the flames and Adela threw the door shut with a clang.*

*The witch's screams rose in waves until it seemed they would send blood streaming from Adela's ears. Adela stumbled back from the hearth, hands cupping the sides of her head. Bastian's face had gone pale and his eyes were streaming as he wrapped an arm around Adela's shoulder.*

*After an eternity, the screams faded and the cottage fell into a dull silence.*

*"Do you think she's dead?" Adela whispered.*

*Bastian took a step back toward the hearth. "We have to find out."*

*He placed a hand on the handle, preparing to pull it open, when the door to the cottage banged open. Adela yelped and spun around. Nicol stood there, naked and furious. Behind him, Adela could just make out the other five villagers who had been previously decorating the witch's garden.*

*"Nicol! Oh, thank the stars!" Adela ran to the man and embraced him. The guard threw his arms around her and buried his head in her shoulder.*

*Bastian cleared his throat and dipped his head toward the others. "Perhaps we can find these folks some blankets."*

*Adela blushed and ran to the chest at the foot of the bed. She pulled out several blankets as well as her own cloak and Bastian's jacket and pack. Passing them around, she received looks of confusion and gratitude, pain and elation. They all– aside from Nicol– had different versions of the same tale to tell. A beautiful voice calling them from their beds to meet an equally beautiful woman. She'd snapped the enchantment on each and marched them through the woods to her cottage where she walked them straight into the hearth. She'd wasted no time with the others as she had with Bastian and Adela. They'd never stood a chance.*

*As night was falling and the villagers were tired and weak, the group decided to wait out the darkness inside the cottage. They agreed to make their way home at first light. Adela portioned out hot stew and warm tea. They slept fitfully if they slept at all.*

*As the light changed from deepest black to peachy lavender, Adela nuzzled closer to Bastian. "We still have to know. For sure."*

*He nodded in agreement. As soon as the others were up and moving, Bastion once again stood beside the heavy hearth door. Nicol and Adela stood to either side of him, Adela with the broom and Nicol with his bow. When Bastian pulled the metal outward, Adela sucked in a breath.*

*There, crouched just within the lip of the hearth, was a figure born of nightmares. Horns and teeth. Claws and scales.*

*A gargoyle demon carved of fine grey marble leered back at them.*

We just got to teeth and claws and it's over? What the actual fuck?

Doria scrubbed at her eyes. She made it through the story and, while it had kept her engaged, the actual plot was just as terrible as she knew it would be. A tangled mess of naked perfect people and the implication of a happy ending.

In the real world, the man would have been all too happy to sacrifice the girl in an effort to free himself, or he would have traded her in for a roll in the hay with the hot witch.

She could not wait to get back to the bookshop the next day and tell Miles Oak how terrible his choice had been.

# 4

**THE** sound of the apartment door opening snapped Doria out of her thoughts and she glanced up to see Felicity entering, her cheeks flushed with the excitement of a night out. The red-haired beauty shook off her coat, spraying water droplets everywhere. Instinctively, Doria moved to shield the book from the onslaught.

"Hey, Peaches," Felicity called, her voice warm as always. If anyone else had dared to call Doria "Peaches" they'd be met with a scowl and more than a few choice words. Not Felicity.

Felicity had been there during "the year of unending feces" when Doria's world fell apart, when she had nowhere to go and no one to turn to. She'd been there to help pick up the pieces. And she'd been there every day since.

"You're up past your bedtime."

Doria sighed, rubbing her tired eyes again. "It's been a day. Let me tell you. First, I spent the afternoon doing my best not to get molested at work, lost a huge tip, got caught in the rain, accused of shoplifting, and finally was coerced into reading this god-awful book by a hunky nerd."

Felicity barked a laugh. "Hunky nerds and bad books, huh? That's on the same list as being molested at work? At least you've got your priorities in order." She narrowed her eyes at Doria. "Let's start with the nerd, shall we?"

Doria couldn't suppress the giggle that bubbled up. She wasn't a giggler by nature, but once again, Felicity brought it out in her. She recounted the events at the bookshop, trying to convey how completely amazing the place was, while also describing the series of small oddities that left her feeling off balance.

"It's called Vespertine Books. You've never heard of it?" she asked as she thumbed the pages of the book.

"Nope. Maybe it's new."

"It didn't seem new. Had that feeling like it's just always been there."

Felicity shrugged and shook her head.

Doria continued the tale where she'd left off. She told Felicity about Miles and the deal they'd struck after she'd accidentally forgotten the expensive leather Poe book was in her bag. She included how angry she'd been when he seemed to imply that she should read romance instead of her stack of horror and how he'd duped her into reading such an abysmal piece of fluff.

"Well it doesn't really sound like he was judging you," Felicity said. "He's probably just used to selling popular books and a lot of women our age read romance."

"Oh, he was totally judging me."

"Whatever you say," Felicity laughed.

"And," Doria continued, "there are tons of popular horror and thriller books out now."

"So just donate the book to the library or something. No one says you have to read the rest of it," Felicity added.

"That's the best part," Doria said with a little smile. "I get to go back there tomorrow and tell him how much I hated it. You know, just for the sake of getting my point across."

"And the fact that he's a 'hunky nerd' has nothing to do with it?" Felicity teased.

"None at all. He's completely not my type. No tats, no piercings. He was wearing tailored pants and a vest for god's sake."

"Mmm-hmm." Felicity gave her a knowing smile.

"What?"

"Maybe you two made this little deal just so you'd have a reason to go back."

"Oh come on Fel. Even if he was my type, you think some guy I just met is interested in me? And the best way he has to show it is by giving me a terrible book to read?"

"Stranger things have happened."

"Well, it's not happening now."

"Doria. Peaches. Honey. The fact of the matter is you need to get laid. We both know this. And if returning to that bookshop gets you closer to that goal, I am 100% on board with this terrible book scheme."

Doria couldn't stifle her full-blown laugh. She stood and carried her dirty soup bowl to the kitchen. "I'm going to bed, you hooligan."

The following day dawned clear and bright. Doria had high hopes for getting through her shift at the café with the same sunny attitude. Those hopes lasted all of about thirteen minutes.

She had just taken an order from a cute couple who sat nestled in the corner when a family of six entered and sat themselves at one of the center tables. As she brought a stack of menus and a pitcher of water to them, one of the kids tipped himself back in his chair and sent it crashing to the floor with him still in it. She rushed over to assist him and, as she did, his frantic father barreled into her, sending the watcher pitcher flying. Chaos ensued and only after several long minutes, a free meal for them all, and some quick use of the mop bucket, could Doria get back to her other tables.

By the time she left for the evening, she was once again exhausted. Cursing the asshole who had convinced her to leave the city and her education behind, as well as herself for allowing him to lead her so far from her goals, she headed toward the part of town where she'd found the hidden bookshop.

It took her awhile to locate the battered wood sign, and she wondered how the place could possibly stay open, cowering as it was between the two larger buildings. She actually passed by it twice and had to retrace her footsteps in order to locate the door.

Shaking her head, she pushed open the entry, the gentle tinkling of the bell announcing her arrival. For the second time, she noticed that there didn't seem to be many other customers in the shop, but she remembered how easily Peter Smith had snuck up on her the previous evening and guessed there might be others deeper in the stacks.

"Ah, Doria! Welcome back," a melodic voice called. Doria turned to see the beautiful older woman in the same place she'd been the night before. Her sharp eyes seemed to study Doria even as she smiled from her place on the overstuffed chair. Doria tried to smile back, but she didn't recall telling the woman her name the last time they'd met and she wondered how she'd learned it. Perhaps Miles had shared the information, but that seemed unlikely. What reason would he have to do so?

"I'm sorry. I guess I didn't catch your name last night," Doria said as she approached and extended her hand.

The dark-haired woman rose and, instead of shaking hands, she wrapped Doria in a warm hug. "I'm so sorry about that. It's Cassondra. But most people call me Cassie."

Doria wasn't sure how to react. She stepped back, arms stiff at her sides. "Nice to meet you, Cassie. Are you a friend of Miles' then?"

"We go way back, he and I." She winked and then gathered up her things from the table in front of her.

As if summoned by the conversation, Miles appeared from one of the shadowy aisles, a book in hand. Doria's heart fluttered as she caught sight of him. He was once again dressed pristinely in a button-down shirt that was open at the neck and cuffed at his wrists. A deep charcoal tight-tailored vest and matching trousers fit him snuggly, and he had on thick black framed glasses, making him look even more scholarly and serious than he had the night before.

Doria's mouth went dry. He was so not her type, but he definitely looked good. Noticing her staring, he removed the glasses with a flourish and grinned at her.

"Don't take them off on my account. You're really rocking the whole Clark Kent vibe here."

"Ah, they're really only for reading. Good to see you again Doria James." She felt heat flood her cheeks at the sound of her name on his lips.

"Likewise." Doria silently cursed herself for not having something witty or scathing to say. She glanced around, taking in the piles of books, looking at everything but him until she could get her stupid hormones to calm down. Maybe Felicity was right and she really did need to get some action.

The shop filled with an uncomfortable silence.

Cassondra cleared her throat.

Doria took a breath. "The book you gave me. I read one of the stories. Sorry I couldn't stomach more than that."

"You made it through one though? That's a start." Miles walked to the counter and shuffled some papers.

Doria reached into her bag a pulled out the thin volume. Cassie looked at it over her shoulder. "That's what he had you read? Interesting."

"I thought she might like it," Miles said mildly.

"And clearly she did not," Cassie added pointedly. "Well, I've got to be going. I'll leave you to your discussion. Hopefully the next story he chooses will suit your taste a bit better, Doria. If not, swing by the library sometime and I'll give you some recommendations."

"You work at the library?" Doria asked.

"I do. Pop in and I'll show you around."

"Are you heading to see Elenor tonight, Cassie?" Miles asked as the pixie-haired beauty made it to the door.

"I am."

"Please give her my best." A sadness crossed his face and Doria wondered who Elenor might be.

"Will do. Goodnight." She slipped out the door, leaving Doria alone with Miles.

He ran a hand through his hair and looked at Doria. The sadness retreated and was replaced by a twinkle of mischief. "Now. Tell me why you hated the book."

Settling into one of the ridiculously comfy overstuffed chairs, she focused her thoughts. She had so many things to say about the story she'd read and she wanted to make sure she got to all of them. Miles dropped down across from her and leaned forward, resting his elbows on his knees as if he really wanted to hear what she had to say.

She didn't want to offend him exactly, but he had to know the story was trash. "I'm kind of surprised you suggested it actually. I tried with the first one in the book, but it was so syrupy, I almost vomited."

He nodded as if he understood. "Yeah, that retelling of Cinderella can be a bit much. So what did you move on to then?"

"*Bastian and Adela*," she said with a sigh. "Really Miles? Sexy Hansel and Gretel? That's your idea of good stuff?"

"Actually, I quite like that one, yes." He smiled at the horror on her face.

"That is insane."

"I don't see how enjoying a sweet little story *Bastian and Adela* is insane."

"It was completely inane and pointless. Forget about the rip-off on a classic tale, all it did was degrade women. Both the heroine and villain were after nothing but sex."

Mile's eyebrows shot up in surprise and Doria noted the slight flush creeping up his neck. She was surprised by his reaction and for a split second worried she'd overstepped by being so candid. He tilted his head in silent contemplation, then leaned back in his chair and smiled while shaking his head.

"Interesting," he mused, his fingers tapping rhythmically against the overstuffed armrest. "And here I thought we might have similar tastes. I guess I misjudged."

"Well now I'm curious. What made you think I'd like it?" Doria asked thoughtfully.

"Your love of stories in general, I suppose," he responded simply. She could feel his gaze in her very bones. "I thought perhaps it might be a nice change of pace from your preferred dark genres."

"Nope. It wasn't."

"Clearly." A rueful smile tugged at his lips. "I do appreciate your candor though. I don't often get to hear what readers think after they've selected a book. Cassie is, of course, an exception, and let me tell you, she has very definite opinions about what she likes. It seems you two share that particular characteristic."

"I don't know about Cassie, but my candor gets me into trouble more than I'd like to admit. I lean toward the horror and dark thrillers because I know it isn't real."

"Neither are most fantasy books."

"True, but the ones I really get into are the stories with a strong female protagonist. Not a girl willing to drop her pants just for a guy with a huge rod."

Miles snorted and Doria smiled at the way she'd caught him off guard.

"Point taken. And to be clear, I'm not saying you're wrong. Everyone reads for different reasons. I learned long ago that, for me, sometimes a story is just a story. They can be extremely powerful tools or they can just be fun and wistful. As long as the reader is getting something out of it that they need in the moment that they're reading it, it's done its job. Even if it's just to take make us forget our troubles and focus on a sweet woman who happens to fall for the guy with the *huge* rod."

He winked at her and she nearly came undone.

"OK fine. I see your point. But really? That story wasn't fun and wistful. Adela was little more than a prop for Bastion's whims and the witch was a caricature of a wicked woman, right down to her naked statue fetish."

"I loved the witch!" he said in mock indignation. "And you missed the part about Adela fighting back against those who sought to control her. She found her own strength and took charge of her destiny. She saved them all. Isn't that a powerful message in its own right?"

"Did we read the same story?" Doria asked incredulously. "Her strength was in following around a man who clearly didn't know her well, despite being lifelong friends."

He held up his hands in surrender. "OK. You win. Maybe I need to find you a good dark romance next."

"Uhhh. No. I'm good thanks."

"Well, I need to redeem myself and send you out of here with something you might like."

"Anything good and gory will do. Just leave the 'throbbing need' out of it."

They sat quietly and, just when Doria felt it was growing uncomfortable, Miles said, "Tell me Doria James, why are you so reluctant to read any sort of romance story? Not just the syrupy ones."

Doria wasn't sure she wanted to answer, but she'd already come this far. "I suppose," she began slowly, "it's because the fictional book boyfriends are always unrealistic. No real man could ever compare to the ones we find in books. And in my experience, it's better not to get your hopes up and wait for something that will never materialize."

As soon as the words left her lips, she felt the smallest pang of regret. She really shouldn't have shared that with Miles. He was a virtual stranger and now he was likely thinking she was a bitter and unhappy woman. Not the best way to start off. But something in the way he was happy to sit and chat with her had brought a comfy kind of intimacy and she'd been drawn in despite herself.

"Ah. I see," he murmured softly. "It's true that the real world can be far more complicated and painful than the world of fiction." They'd only just met, but Doria couldn't ignore the tightness around his eyes.

"So," she forced lightness into her voice. "You like romance novels, huh? There's got to be a story there. I figured you for a classics and epics kind of guy."

He smiled and rubbed the bridge of his nose. "I do in fact love most of the classics. Except for Wuthering Heights. I loathe that book. As to how I got into romance, well. . . I think that might be a story for another day." He paused and added with a wink, "After you've read a few more romantasies, that is."

Doria couldn't contain the laugh that bubbled up, the tension in the room dissipating. She leaned back and rested her head on the overstuffed chair, an unfamiliar feeling seeping over her. Contentment? It had been so long since she just felt. . . content.

"This place is such an escape. You must love coming to work here each day."

Miles looked at her with a sad smile. "Some days are better than others."

Doria wasn't ready to leave the shop just yet. She asked Miles about his favorite books of all time, then shared some of hers. They had *very* different lists. She agreed to read some of his favorites eventually and, to her surprise, he'd already read most of the ones she suggested. He must have a lot of time on his hands.

Doria shifted in her seat, deciding to change the subject. "So, Cassondra seems great. She must be in here a lot." Strangely enough, not a single other patron had entered the shop the entire time they'd been embroiled in conversation.

"She shows up whenever she's able."

"And Elenor? An ex-girlfriend perhaps?" Her tone was light and teasing, but she couldn't deny the faint twinge of curiosity that spurred the question.

Miles threw back his head and laughed until tears trailed down his cheeks. Doria was clearly missing the joke. "Oh. No," he said, wiping a tear from his eye. "Far from an ex as you can get. We've also been close for years. She's something like sister to me. Did I mention she also happens to be in her eighties?"

"I see." Doria nodded, feeling more than a little foolish. She toyed with the edges of her sleeve.

"She's actually quite amazing. Kind of a resident expert on town history and folklore and a wonderful human being. You might really enjoy talking with her."

"That might be fun. Sure." Doria looked to the front of the store and realized it was quite dark outside. "I should be getting home. It's late."

She didn't want the evening to end. The smell of paper and ink, the plush armchairs, the great conversation with a seriously attractive man—it was the closest thing to a date she'd had in a long while. But she couldn't just sleep on the floor of the shop either.

Miles seemed to sense her reluctance. He shot her a knowing smile and, without speaking, he stood and crossed to one of the towering bookshelves. His fingers danced over the spines, clearly seeking one title in particular. He found it with practiced ease and pulled it free from its spot on the shelf. Once again his fingers lingered on the back of her hand as he handed her the book. "Here," he said. His voice as gentle as feathers brushing against her skin. "Read the third story in the collection. I think you'll find it more to your liking."

Doria hesitated, her fingers tracing the embossed letters on the cover. "Why not just let me choose my own story? Why go to the trouble of selecting them for me?"

"Because," Miles replied quietly, his gaze holding hers with a quiet intensity that sent shivers down her spine. "Books have the power to change us, heal us, show us worlds, and people, and attitudes we never knew existed. And sometimes, when we least expect it, they can bring people together as well." He stepped back, releasing her from the magnetic pull of his stare. "Enjoy the story, Doria James. I'll see you soon."

With a final lingering look at Miles' chiseled jaw and bright blue eyes, Doria slipped the book into her bag and left the shop. She couldn't shake the feeling that something profound had shifted within her—that the course of her life was being subtly rewritten by some unseen hand. As the night deepened around her, she found herself eager for the first time in a long time. Eager to discover where the next chapter would lead.

# 5

**DORIA** raced home, driven by the need to see what sort of story Miles had chosen for her. Felicity was still out. Both of them were off the following day and they'd made plans to hang out together, but Doria knew her friend wouldn't be home for hours, which meant she could read late into the night and probably still be out of bed and ready to go before Felicity even cracked an eyelid.

She dropped her things by the door, opened a bottle of wine, and got situated on the couch without even breaking stride.

The cover of this one was also well done, but it had a slightly edgier feel to it—the font was jagged and dramatic, despite the fancy embossing. It might have been some sort of special edition.

The spine creaked open like it was sharing a secret just with her, and Doria quickly flipped to the third story in the volume. Immediately, she had higher hopes for this one. A few pages in, she realized it was another fairytale retelling—a modern take on Little Red Riding Hood.

At least the title was better.

## Seeing Red

*Most nights, Corina was happy to be in the woods. She liked the smell of the pine, the sound of the wind, and the feel of the damp earth beneath her feet. She was aware of the nocturnal predators about, but they rarely bothered her. Most were after smaller prey, and those big enough to give her pause could be easily evaded. That was most nights.*

*Tonight was different. Tonight was a hunter's moon.*

*On the hunter's moon, Corina wanted nothing more than to be tucked up in her cozy little apartment with the view of the river below— a good book in her hands and a glass of pinot within arm's reach.*

Doria paused, looked between the book and her glass of

wine, and smiled to herself.

*So, when her phone had lit up with a text message from her mother earlier that day, she thought about just ignoring the request that it contained. Except nothing from her mother was ever a request. No matter how nicely it was worded. Beneath the surface, it was always an order. Do this or else. Corina loved and respected her mother, but she'd also seen what could happen if a request went unanswered. Corina didn't need to be asked twice.*

*The request was simple enough. One of The Den's guests was interested in an evening hiking excursion and needed a guide. It wasn't completely unheard of. Birdwatchers and nature lovers came to the little inn for just these types of experiences. Unplug and get off the grid for a day or two. Most of them thought of themselves as adept* adventurers, but Corina's mother, Bess, knew how easy it was to get lost in the dense forest at night and always insisted they have a guide if going out near sunset. Corina took her mother's guests out several nights a week. But never on a hunter's moon.

When she'd texted her mother back to remind her of the day, the reply had been immediate. 'I know it's not ideal. Just be here early. Moonrise isn't until 9:00. You'll be fine.'

Easy for her to say.

As there was no sense in arguing, Corina did as her mother requested. She'd dressed in her cargo pants, a white tank, and her most comfortable hiking boots. Then she grabbed her favorite red all-weather jacket and her pack and headed up the hill to The Den.

Corina parked her battered Jeep in the side drive and mounted the porch steps. The sun still hadn't set, but she felt an anxious itch beneath her skin. The sooner this excursion started, the sooner it'd be over. Then maybe she'd rest a little easier. Just as she was about to open the door, the sound of tires on the drive snagged her attention. Turning, she blew out a long and heavy breath.

Well shit. This night just could not get any worse.

"Hey there Corina." Kyle Cobern stepped out of the white and green Bronco he drove all over town. He wasn't wearing a uniform, but that didn't mean he wasn't on duty.

"Hey Kyle. What's up?" She tried to sound calm and indifferent, but if the deputy had made it all the way up there to The Den, there had to be a reason. He generally avoided the place like the plague. Despite her mother's denial, Corina always thought Kyle had something against Bess.

"You going out there tonight?" He nodded toward the thick expanse of pine and cedar encroaching on the back of the inn.

"That was the plan. Mom's got a guest who wants a little adventure."

*He rubbed his hand across the back of his neck and shook his head.*

*"Is that a problem, Deputy?" Corina had a hard time keeping the disdain from her voice. In all the years she'd known Kyle, she'd never taken a liking to him. It wasn't anything she could put her finger on, but he made her skin crawl. Every now and then she'd catch him looking at her with a hunger in his eyes, which was flat-out disgusting, considering he was old enough to be her father.*

*"We've had some reports of what sounds like wolves in the area. Not sure it's smart for you to be out there after nightfall."*

*The reports didn't surprise her. She knew what lurked out there. What she couldn't work out was why Kyle would care enough to make the trek up the hill with the information.*

*"And?" she prodded.*

*"And we got a report of a missing hiker this morning. The girl isn't local. Just a backpacker on her way through with friends. The group said she went out early this morning to commune with nature and never made it back to the campsite. We've had teams out all afternoon looking for her. Nothing turned up yet."*

*"Well. I'll keep my eyes open. Who knows, maybe I can help."*

*"Suit yourself. But don't say I didn't warn you." Kyle headed back toward his car. He threw a hand up as he opened the door but didn't turn around. "Let your mom know I said hi."*

*Corina's stomach flipped over as she watched Kyle turn in the drive and head back down the hill. Once his brake lights were gone, she'd finally collected herself enough to pull open the door and go in search of the hiker she was taking out into the woods.*

*When Corina found them, her mother was waiting in the kitchen, one eyebrow raised as she glanced at her watch.*

*Beside her stood a tall, well-built man roughly the same age as Corina. His dark chocolate hair hung to his shoulders. He had a full beard– thankfully clean and well-trimmed. Corina hated the scraggly look. He wore a blue flannel shirt untucked from his jeans. Corina glanced to his shoes and was pleased to see that they were both good quality and well-worn in.*

*"About time," her mother said pointedly.*

*"Sorry. I got caught up outside talking with Kyle Cobern".*

*"What in god's name was he doing here?" Bess started and then seemed to realize she didn't want to know. "Never mind. Corina, this is Liam Grey. Liam, my daughter Corina. No one knows these woods like she does. I hope you find all that you're looking for. At the very least, the evening should be memorable."*

*"Thank you, Bess." His voice was a deep rumble. "I've been looking forward to this for some time now." He turned toward Corina and nodded. A shiver ran down her spine. She wasn't sure she'd ever seen eyes quite like his– the palest blue imaginable, surrounded by a thin ring of slate.*

*"We should be going, Mr. Grey. The light will be fading soon, and I'd like to be back before it's too late."*

*"Please, call me Liam."*

*"Right. Liam, then. Have you got everything? Water, flashlight?" she asked. Her mother usually provided guests with a list of supplies to take out with them, but she liked to check, just to make sure.*

*Liam patted the small waterproof pack at his side. "All right here," he said before slinging it onto his back and following her toward the exit off the back of the kitchen.*

*"So, is there anything in particular you're looking for?"*

*"In life or on this hike?" The way he asked, she wasn't sure if it was meant as a joke or not.*

*"The hike. Most people don't want to wander around in the dark unless they're after something."*

*"I'm not sure that what I'm after will be out there."* Interesting. *"But you never know. Just a general lay of the land would be great. I'm staying for a few days, and if I can convince you're mother I won't kill myself, I plan to do more exploring on my own while I'm here."*

*They'd made it to the edge of the trees and a small narrow break in the foliage which marked the path Corina normally took away from the inn and farther into the forest.*

*"I wouldn't bet on it. She's pretty serious when it comes to the safety of her guests."* Most nights, at least. *"Just because I show you around for an hour or two, doesn't mean you won't get turned around out here by yourself tomorrow."*

*She could feel him behind her. "We'll see."* Another shiver ran up Corina's spine.

*She set a course toward a few handy landmarks just in case the man decided to explore again on his own. She showed him the large cedar that had been split by lightning several years ago, a small rocky outcrop covered in lime green lichen, and the place where the creek split before trailing off further down the hill. Liam took in each landmark with his eerie blue eyes as he studied the forest around him. Several times Corina had to look behind her to make sure she hadn't lost him. The man moved through the forest with near silent ease. Each time she checked however, he was close behind her.*

*"If all else fails, listen for the river. You can hear it off in the distance when it's quiet. Follow the sound downhill and eventually you'll come to the banks. From there, it's a half day in either direction before you hit civilization. It isn't perfect, but it might save your life if it comes down to it."*

*Liam lifted one corner of his mouth in a half smile. "Thank you. I really don't plan on getting lost though."* The silvery light had faded to a deeper plum shade and Corina glanced at her watch.

"Shit," Corina spat, and Liam huffed at her choice of words. "Sorry. But we really need to be getting back."

Her skin itched with nerves. She hadn't meant to lose track of the time, but it had been a nice quiet hike. Liam had easily kept up and she had ventured deeper than she had planned.

Corina pulled the flashlight from her own pack and moved to start back toward the inn when Liam reached out and grabbed her arm. All of a sudden, he was much closer than she'd expected, their bodies almost touching. He looked down at her upturned face. Another tingle ran through her.

"What's out here that you're afraid of?" His voice was barely more than a whisper, but she felt the deep timber of it all the way in her toes.

She opened her mouth and then slammed it shut as a long, low howl filled the air around them

"Shit," Corina said again. She looked up at the sky even as her feet began moving back toward the inn. "How fast can you run?"

"It was just a wolf, right?" Liam asked as he kept pace beside her, their twin flashlight beams bobbing ahead of them in the gloom. He didn't seem worried, only a little bemused by the idea.

"Something like that." Corina scanned the trees and began jogging faster, easily pulling in front of him to guide their way back. Her feet knew the paths, the dips, the hollows, and where the low-lying branches hung. She'd love to sprint all out, but Liam would get left behind. On a hunter's moon, leaving him on his own could prove deadly.

She checked over her shoulder and was happy to see him easily keeping up. In fact, he didn't seem affected at all by the brisk jog.

*Another mournful howl filled the air around them. Just as it was cutting off, a series of answering howls rose in crescendo. Corina felt her skin tingling and instinctively pushed her body to run faster. They needed to be inside. Corina needed to be inside. What the hell had her mother been thinking when she arranged for this evening hike? And why had Corina agreed?*

*They were just coming up to the large split cedar, the inn another quarter of a mile ahead through the trees, when a gunshot rang out. Corina stumbled at the sound and Liam caught her elbow, helping to keep her on her feet.*

*"They allow hunting this close to the town?" Liam asked. The trail had widened up and he was running even with her now, no longer following in her wake. He was barely out of breath despite the solid ten minutes of running they'd been doing.*

*"Not usually, but tonight is different." Corina looked toward the east. The trees blocked the horizon but she thought she could just make out the glow of the moonrise. "The inn is just ahead. Probably another 600 yards or so. Stay on the trail and you'll be there in no time. Get inside. Mom will be waiting."*

*"What about you?" His pale eyes assessed her in the dark. Her body shuddered.*

*"I need to check on something. Don't look so concerned. I'll be fine."*

*Corina didn't give him a chance to argue or ask further questions. She veered off the path and headed toward the downslope and a path that would bring her closer to the road.*

Doria smiled to herself, impressed by the fierce female lead who refused to be the victim. Not a kindred spirit exactly, but at least someone she could root for.

*Corina could smell the night blooming around her. Another set of howls echoed off the trees. Closer now. Heart racing in her chest, she stopped when she saw lights up ahead.*

*There was a small turnout along one side of the road. During the day, hikers and campers used the spot to park and then head off into the beauty of the woods. Tonight, however, the small space was filled with an assortment of trucks, jeeps, and sheriff's cars. Several of the vehicles sat dark, but two or three— including Kyle's rig— had their headlights shining into the trees.*

*Between the missing hiker, the reports of wolves in the area, and the hunter's moon, Kyle and his group would be on edge. Corina knew the night was about to get ugly and while she wanted nothing more than to be cuddled up safe and warm inside, she couldn't allow them to kill some poor innocent creature in the name of misguided justice. She hadn't heard any further gunshots. Silently, she hoped that one had missed its mark. She needed to lead them away before any more opportunities at a target arose.*

*Hunching down behind a thick set of brambles, Corina crept closer to where the cars were parked. She imagined the men and women from those vehicles had swept out in some sort of an arc, but she wanted to be sure. The last thing she needed was to get caught before her plan took effect. Stilling herself in the shadows, she tilted her head and listened. The sound of voices could be heard in the space around her. They didn't sound too far out yet. She glanced down at her watch. She had just enough time.*

*Corina unzipped her red jacket and folded it neatly before shoving it, along with the rest of her clothes, deep beneath the brambles. Looking skyward, she inhaled deeply. The night air tasted like honey and power. Her skin itched and she welcomed the delicious tingle of it. Throwing her head back, she invited the night and the moonbeams. A heartbeat later, her wolf— sleek and grey— emerged, and she set off toward the hunters.*

*Thankfully, Liam was safe at the inn. She could only imagine what he would have done if he'd witnessed her transformation. If she'd been inside, she would have been able to control the shifting, but outside, under the full and glorious hunter's moon, she was at the mercy of the magic in her blood. Her mother knew that, and still she'd sent her out into the woods with a stranger.*

*If Corina was fast on two legs, she was blinding on four. In seconds she was up the embankment and among the vehicles on the road. Sniffing around the trucks, it was easy to decipher the number of hunters in the forest. She caught eight distinct scents, five of which she could quickly identify as folks from town. Throwing her head back, she loosed a howl that was in no way mournful or sad. It was a challenge and a triumph all in one. Then, padding back and forth on the asphalt, she waited until she could hear all eight sets of feet crashing back toward her.*

*It took longer than she would have expected. They must have been farther into the woods than she thought. After several long minutes, she was sure they were close. She howled again and tore off across the road to the edge of the forest on the other side. She waited there, watching for any sign of danger.*

*Kyle was the first to emerge onto the road. His face was flushed and his expression grim. Corina could smell the anger and frustration rolling off of him in waves. She took just a moment to stare at him before loping off into the trees. She was sure to make enough noise so that he could easily follow. She had no intention of letting him catch her, but she needed to keep him busy on her trail for at least a few hours.*

*Corina knew these woods well, but so did Kyle. Each time she thought she might have lost him, he'd turn up behind her again. After a while, she began to hear the voices and movements of the others in Kyle's party. With any luck, they'd all made their way to her side of the road. She led them farther into the pines.*

*The game soon became a bore. Too many times she drew them in just to dance away again. The minutes drew out into hours and Corina found herself ready to go home and go to bed. She began tracking back toward The Den. If she could get close enough, she might be able to shift back and sneak inside without Kyle or his hunters any the wiser.*

*She was within minutes of the inn when a branch snapped off to her left and the strong scent of cheap aftershave wafted to her. Instinctively, the wolf moved to her right and down into a shallow ravine. She felt the trap before she saw it– a circle of hunters closing around her. Thinking of bed, she'd let her guard down and allowed herself to be surrounded. Snarling, she looked for a gap in the ring of bodies.*

*Kyle stepped forward and raised what appeared to be a tranquilizer rifle to his shoulder. She snapped her jaws at him.*

*She didn't want to bite him, but if that's what it took to get out of this mess, she'd do it.*

*"Easy now," the deputy crooned.*

*Corina snarled at him in response and lowered her head. A low growl rumbled out of her as she moved back. If that dart hit her, who knew what might happen.*

*"Can't have you getting away now." Kyle took just a beat to get her in his sights. She smelled his excitement and watched as his finger curled on the trigger.*

*Out of nowhere, an enormous black shape hurled from the shadows and slammed into Kyle, knocking him to the ground. The moving shadow sprang up and Corina was amazed to see it was a dazzling black wolf. It was the biggest animal she'd ever seen.*

*The collision threw the other hunters into motion, but they were sloppy and chaotic.*

*Corina and the black wolf wasted no time. While Kyle clambered to his feet, they sprinted off into the trees and back toward the safety of the inn.*

Werewolves she could work with. As long as there was no alpha-hole business about to go down, Doria thought she might actually end up liking this one.

*Bess was standing on the porch of The Den as Corina raced out of the trees, the large black wolf just steps behind. Corina slowed but didn't dare run through the open door. Not with the unknown wolf so close. She whirled and cut the black beast off before he could get close to the steps or her mother.*

*Corina's mother just clucked her tongue. "Get in here." When Corina growled at the other wolf, her mother added, "Him too."*

*Corina didn't understand why her mother was being so welcoming, but she almost didn't care. She was tired and hungry and wanted nothing more than for this night to end. If Kyle caught up to her now, she wasn't sure what would happen. He certainly would have questions about Bess holding the door open for two large wild animals.*

*Bounding up the steps, she brushed past her mother and into the foyer. As soon as the night sky was obstructed, she could feel control flooding back into her body. She surveyed the downstairs rooms and seeing no one up and about at this hour, she shifted back into her human form.*

*Her mother closed the door and locked it, dimming the interior lights before leading the black wolf into the kitchen. Grabbing a robe kept in the entry closet for just such occasions, Corina followed. Her mother had seen her naked countless times, but that didn't mean she needed to parade around in her birthday suit for the hell of it.*

*She was tying the belt as she strode into the kitchen. "Got one of those for me?" a deep voice rumbled.*

*Corina's head snapped up, her eyes finding a very amused and very naked Liam leaning back against the kitchen counter.*

And...there it was. The naked dude. Doria sighed but continued to read.

He seemed completely at ease; arms folded across a chest lightly dusted with dark hair. He was making zero attempts to cover himself and Corina felt her eyes drift over him before she glanced around the room, looking for the large black wolf. All she saw was a discarded pack and flashlight next to a set of ripped jeans and a tattered flannel.

"Just kidding. I've got clothes upstairs." He smiled at her and made his way to the back stairwell.

Corina spun on her mother. "Did you know?"

Bess blew out a long breath. "No. I didn't sense anything until he came crashing into the house without you. He held off the change for quite a while, but I don't think his control is quite as good as yours." She nodded to the pile of ruined clothing. "You didn't sense it either, I take it?"

Corina shook her head. "It never occurred to me. I guess I should have suspected. He kept up better than most out there."

'Hmm. What happened to you anyway? I thought I'd given you plenty of time to get out and back." Corina was still irritated at her mother's lack of judgment but elected to keep quiet on the topic.

"Kyle Cobern and his band of fucking hunters. I heard a gunshot and was worried they were going after one of the kids." The kids were a small pack of wolves that inhabited the area and held a special place in her heart. She'd watched them on and off for several years and not once had they ever caused problems. They kept to the wilds mostly, but tonight the howls had seemed closer to the inn than they'd ever been. "There was a hiker who went missing and he's blaming it on wolves."

"Asshole." Her mother stated.

"Agreed. Anyway, I wasn't going to be able to hold off for much longer and didn't think your guest would appreciate me going full werewolf in front of him, so…" She shrugged.

Liam was still buttoning up his new shirt as he walked back into the kitchen. "I wouldn't have minded full werewolf." He smirked. When she stared back at him blankly, the smirk died. "I guess we need to talk."

A loud banging came at the front door.

*Corina's mother plastered a broad, pained grimace on her face. "I'm guessing that'll be our fearless deputy. Why don't you two head upstairs and out of sight? It'll be easier to play dumb if it's just me."*

*As she headed to the front of the house, Liam and Corina went up the back stairs to his rented room. Corina followed him inside and sat down at the small dressing table while Liam perched on the end of the bed, elbows on his knees and studying the floor between his bare feet. If Corina expected him to launch into a full-blown explanation about why he was there, she was mistaken.*

*"So. You want to explain yourself, or am I to assume it's just a coincidence that you happen to be a wolf shifter and happen to be here on a little getaway in the middle of nowhere? And you happen to have requested a night hike on a hunter's moon."*

*He looked up at her from under his lashes. "I'd heard some stories and I thought I'd come to check them out for myself."*

*When he didn't elaborate, Corina's temper flared. "That's it? That's all you have to say for yourself? You'd heard some stories?" She stood from the chair and stalked over to him. "I have never met someone like me before. Never. And you just show up out of the blue. How is that even possible?"*

*He sat up straighter on the bed and pierced her with his icy blue eyes. "What do you mean you've never met someone like you? Your mother isn't a shifter?"*

*"No. She's just a tough old cookie who runs a small inn."*

*"Really?" Liam still looked skeptical.*

*"Really."*

*He cocked his head and studied her a moment. "Then how exactly have you learned to control your magic? You should have been on all fours as soon as it got dark out there."*

*"Believe me, when I was a kid, I would have been. My mom had to keep me locked up in a cage during any full moon, not just a strong one like the hunter's."*

*"In a cage. That's disgusting." His face had gone dark.*

*"Yeah well, it was necessary. It's only been within the last few years that I've been able to really control myself. Some nights, if I'm inside, I don't shift at all."*

*"And you like that?" He lifted a single dramatic eyebrow.*

Raised voices sounded from downstairs and Corina wondered what Kyle was accusing her mother of now. Surely there was no way for him to know it had been Corina he'd nearly darted with the tranquilizer.

"Sometimes." She swallowed the bitter lie. She told herself she liked it because it was safe, but deep in her bones, she always longed to be outside. Even when the moon was high and full.

"So, your mother isn't a shifter. Does she have other earth magic?"

"Like what? A witch? Sorry to disappoint, but no. Not that I know of."

"What about your father?"

Corina was starting to lose her temper even further. "I have no idea. I've never met him. Look. Are we done talking about me yet? I want to know why you're here."

Liam licked his lips, a predatory gleam in his eyes. "I thought it was obvious. I came here for you."

The simple statement, combined with the fierce animalistic look from Liam, had Corina backing up a step.

Liam didn't move from his seat on the edge of the bed, but Corina still felt as if he were stalking her. The dark strands of his long hair and beard framed his ice and slate eyes, making him look every bit the wolf he was.

"Afraid?" The word was a harsh whisper, but again, Corina felt it through her entire soul.

Knowing her voice would likely betray her, she shook her head but didn't speak.

"You should be," Liam stated. "But not of me. I might be a wolf, but I'm not the monster in this particular story."

The bizarre statement had Corina finding her voice at last. "Explain."

She leaned up against the door frame, thankful that Liam hadn't shut it when he followed her in minutes earlier.

"I'll tell you what I can– what I suspect. But you need to know, I have just as many questions right now as answers." He paused, seeming to weigh his words. "I think someone is hunting you."

*The sound of the front door slamming echoed up the stairs and into the small bedroom.*

*"And I don't think we should talk about it here," he added.*

*"I'm sure mom has gotten rid of Kyle. She's good at that."*

*"Still. I'd be more comfortable meeting somewhere else. You look like you could use some rest anyway," he said.*

*Corina smirked. "Just what a girl likes to hear. 'You look tired' is code for 'you look like shit'."*

Doria snorted a laugh. She could so completely relate to the sentiment.

*Liam chuckled and Corina thought it was a sound she could get used to.*

*Bess appeared at the top of the stairs. Her face was flushed and her jaw tight, but at least Kyle wasn't tromping up behind her.*

*"I got rid of him, but it wasn't easy." She ran a hand through her hair. "He's convinced I'm hiding something but seemed reluctant to say just what. Anyway, the sun'll be up in an hour or two. You should eat something and then head home and get some rest."*

*Corina's mom knew how much energy she spent when in her wolf form and always had homemade granola, yogurt, or other high-calorie foods on hand. That morning it was a pan full of scrambled eggs laced with at least half a block of cheddar cheese and thick slices of sourdough toast. She'd made enough for both Corina and Liam and the pair devoured every last bit before helping her clean up.*

*As the sun began to stream through the blinds, Corina gathered her things to head home. "Give me your phone and*

*I'll punch in my number. You can call me later after you've gotten some sleep."*

*She ignored her mother's raised brows as she handed the cell back to him.*

*Corina's life had never been typical. She'd been shifting with the moon since she was a baby. She didn't understand why or how it happened, just that it was something other people did not do. She'd learned not to speak of it as a young child. In her adolescent years, she'd tried to look online for others like herself or research what it meant. She'd only been successful in finding horror movies or paranormal romance novels, nothing that actually helped her. As a young adult, she'd made peace with her nature and that was when she'd gained some amount of control over the magic of the transformation.*

*Liam's cryptic statement about being hunted left her confused more than anything. The night had thrown her for a loop in more ways than one, and as she made her way back down the hill, she couldn't shake the feeling that her life was about to get very interesting.*

*After a quick shower, sleep claimed Corina hard and fast.*

*The sound of her favorite Creedence Clearwater Revival tune jolted her awake sometime later. Fumbling for her cell, she answered the unfamiliar number.*

*"Did I wake you?" Liam's voice held a trace of its own yawn.*

*"Yep. You did."*

*"Sorry, but I was hoping to meet up before it gets dark."*

*"Don't apologize. Makes sense. I can meet you at The Den. It'll just take me a few to clean up and make it up the hill."*

*"I'd rather not. Can I come to yours?" He wasn't demanding, only straight forward.*

*She knew she shouldn't agree, but if Liam had meant to harm her, he easily could have done it out in the woods the night before. "Sure. I'll send you the address."*

*Thirty minutes later she was opening the door to the wolf.*

*"Can I get you a drink?"*

*"Sure. I'll take whatever you've got."*

*Liam made himself comfortable on the small sofa while Corina grabbed a couple of beers from her fridge. She handed him one and placed some chips and salsa on the coffee table before settling into her favorite spot– the armchair with the view of the river.*

*He took a long draw on the bottle of amber ale before resting it between his legs and leaning back to look at her.*

*"OK Liam. Talk."*

*"I'm trying to decide where to start. You've really been alone in this your whole life?" He still seemed skeptical.*

*"Well, not alone. I've had my mom."*

*"But she isn't a wolf." The statement sounded half question and half argument as if the very idea was ludicrous.*

*"We've done this already."*

*"I know but… that's just…amazing."*

*"It's not amazing. It's just life."*

*"Of course it's amazing. You think many people could watch their baby turn into a wild animal and not freak out a little bit? You're lucky she didn't drown you in the river for a demon or something. She must have known what to expect when it happened the first time." Corina couldn't argue with him. She'd had the same thought countless times before.*

*"Yeah. I guess." Memories flashed through her one after another. Her mother's terrified eyes as she locked the cage every full moon. Her mother turning her back and leaving the room as a tiny Corina rocked and cried, scared of*

*what she knew was coming. Of her mother threatening to drive her out into the woods and leave her there if she ever told anyone what she was.*

*Her mom was tough, she reminded herself. She'd dealt with things in her own way and Corina had convinced herself she was stronger for it.*

*"Look. I was raised by parents who are both wolves. They knew what they were getting into when they had me, and still, I struggled growing up. I've known you for less than a day and I can tell you're something special." He looked down at his beer as he thought about what to say next. "I wonder who gave that gift to you."*

*"What do you mean? Who my dad is?"*

*"He must have been pretty powerful. It won't be long before others come looking for you, if they aren't already. We are rare, Corina. The kind of power you have over your magic is rarer still. If I could track you down based on whispers and stories, so can others. I came here for two reasons. The first was because there have been whispers of a hunter searching for a lone wolf. Someone out there wants to put you back in a cage." Corina didn't think she was imagining the concern in his voice.*

*"What was the other reason?"*

*He took another long drink from his beer before he placed it on the table next to the untouched snacks. He rose and walked over to where she was sitting and sank down onto his haunches before taking her hand in his. "I came here to see what kind of threat you would be to our kind. The last thing we need is for some lone wolf bringing hunters down on us all. But I realize now, I don't need to worry. You are more than capable of fending for yourself. When I saw you moving through the forest last night... I've never seen anyone move like you. Strong. Confident. Graceful. Both on two feet and four. I thought I'd need to convince you to come home with me. To instruct you. To keep you safe. Clearly, that is not the case. I feel like a complete ass for even entertaining the thought."*

*He squeezed her hand briefly then rose and paced back toward the sofa.*

*"Nice speech," Corina teased. "I thought for a second there you might kiss me."*

*"Would you have let me?"*

*"Maybe you should come over here and find out."*

# 6

DORIA rolled her eyes. Here it comes. The sweaty sex. The over-the-top descriptions. The lover, more beast than man, who could make a woman orgasm multiple times with his amazing sexual skills.

*The kiss was everything Corina hoped it would be. Confident. Seductive. And just the tiniest bit predatory. Liam's hands framed her face as he captured her breath right along with her lips. Corina found herself not only leaning into him but making a strangled moaning sound she was quite sure she'd never made before.*

*Liam pulled back and grinned down at her. "That was unexpected."*

*"I don't like to be predictable."*

*"Clearly." The light in the room was infused with amber as the sun began its descent over the trees. It cast a wicked gleam in his eyes as he looked at her. Liam ran his tongue over his bottom lip and Corina resisted the urge to reach her fingers up to trail its progress.*

*Instead, she pushed him back toward the sofa and followed him down until she was sitting in his lap. She trailed kisses from his lips down his jaw, giggling at the tickle of his beard under her lips. Her fingers were bunched in the front of his shirt. Taking a breath, she looked down at the buttons. "Can I?"*

*He nodded and she began unfastening them one at a time. The hard planes of his chest and abdomen came into view little by little. Although she'd seen him the night before, she was still in awe of the sheer perfection of his build. He sat forward and allowed her to tug the fabric down his sculpted arms. She ran her hands over the dark hair dusted over him and smiled.*

*Even though they'd only just met, something about Liam drew Corina in. Maybe it was the wolf in him. Maybe it was her loneliness. Or maybe it was just the astounding way that he looked at her. It didn't matter. She only knew she wanted to be here with him at this moment.*

*Liam seemed to feel the same way. He welcomed her hands and her lips, letting her control things at her own pace.*

*After several more delicious minutes, Corina pushed herself back from him but kept her fingers twined in his hair. She was nearly breathless but needed to slow things down before it went too far too fast.*

*"So," she cleared her throat. "What am I supposed to do now? Go into hiding? Come join your pack?"*

*Her tone was light. She didn't really think he had a pack, but he had meant to do something when he tracked her down.*

*"Is now the best time to talk about this?" he asked.*

*"No probably not, but I like to multi-task."*

*He smiled and ran a hand over her jaw to the line of her collarbone. "Fair enough. I'm not sure you need to do anything. I meant it when I said that you surprised me. You aren't the lone wolf I expected. But someone gave you your gift Corina. Aren't you interested in figuring out about your family? You could start there. I could help you."*

*"You don't even know me."*

*"No. I don't. But I'd like to."*

*Corina was opening her mouth to either respond or to kiss him again when her phone began vibrating. Expecting her mother, she picked it up and was surprised to see Kyle Coburn's number on the screen. She debated letting it go to voicemail, but something in her gut told her to answer it.*

*Pulling herself from Liam's lap, she frowned. "I better get this."*

*"Of course." He ran a hand through his dark locks and leaned back further into the sofa cushions.*

Huh? No actual sex? For real? Doria flipped ahead a few pages and frowned. Not that she was looking forward to an overly descriptive pages-long porn passage or anything, but at this point, she thought Corina deserved to have some fun.

*Hitting the green button as she walked from the sofa, Corina answered. "Deputy."*

*"Listen Corina and don't argue. Before I go on, I need to know— is that bastard Liam Grey with you?" Kyle's voice was full of authority. Something was definitely not right.*

*If anyone was a bastard, she was pretty sure it was Kyle, not Liam.*

*"Yes." She didn't elaborate, wanting to see what this was about before she let Liam in on the conversation.*

*"OK. If you can, I'm going to need you to act as if nothing is wrong. I don't want him running again, but Corina, listen to me. He's dangerous. Real dangerous."*

*"Go on."*

*"I just got word that he's wanted for the suspected killing of a girl upstate. The guys leading the manhunt tracked him here. To The Den."*

*Corina's heart rate kicked up. She glanced over at the man whom she'd just been kissing. He looked completely at ease. Not at all like a man wanted for murder. But what did a murderer look like? She had no idea.*

*"That's not all. I'm worried about Bess."*

*"Mom? Why? What does she have to do with this?" Corina couldn't keep her voice level and she saw Liam flick his eyes toward her, a small furrow forming in his brow.*

*"I've been trying to get through to her all afternoon and she isn't answering. I'm sending some men that way now."*

*Corina thought back to her earlier conversation with Liam. She had wanted to meet him at the inn, but he'd insisted on coming here instead. Had he done something to her mother?*

*"I need to get up there."*

*"That's not a good idea Corina. I'm–"*

*Corina didn't hear what Kyle was going to say next as she disconnected the call. None of this made sense and she couldn't think while she was talking to the deputy. His accusations didn't feel true, but what reason could he have to lie to her? She just needed to get up the hill and check on her mother herself. Then all of this could be sorted. Kyle said Liam was dangerous, but he'd had more than enough time to harm her if that was his intention.*

*Looking at Liam, she saw real concern on his face. "Are you ok? Who was on the phone?"*

*"I have to go." She was already sprinting to the door even as he was rising from the couch and trying to button his shirt at the same time.*

*"Hey." He grabbed her wrist. "Corina. Slow down."*

*She wrenched her arm free as she opened the door. Liam was right behind her and had the presence of mind to pull the door shut behind him.*

*She made it out to the small parking space in front of her building and froze. Liam's truck was parked behind her Jeep. The tires on both vehicles had been slashed. It seemed as though neither of them was going anywhere.*

*"What the fuck is going on?" Liam slid to a halt next to her, his eyes bouncing from the slashed tires to Corina and back again. "Who was on the phone, Corina?"*

*When she didn't immediately answer, he sighed, "Whatever it is, I only want to help. You can trust me."*

*Wasting time would do no good. Either Kyle was telling the truth or he wasn't. She didn't think Liam would go to the trouble of slashing his own tires, which meant someone else wanted to keep them here, away from the inn and her mother.*

*"It was Kyle, the deputy who was in charge last night. He said he's been having trouble getting a hold of my mom and that you might have something to do with that."*

*He frowned. "Why would I have anything to do with your mom?"*

*"Well, according to Kyle, you may or may not be a wanted man," Corina replied.*

*"If I'm wanted, it's news to me."*

*"He says you killed a girl."*

*Liam frowned. "You don't believe him, do you?"*

*"Honestly, Liam, I don't know what I believe. I only know something isn't right, and I need to get up the hill and check in at The Den."*

*"Well then, let's go."*

*"Umm..." she dipped her head toward the cars.*

*"It can't be, what? Five miles max?"*

*Corina nodded. "About that, yeah."*

*Liam walked back toward the porch, slipping his shirt back off as he went. She looked at him before realizing what he was planning. "You're going to shift?"*

*"Yep. And so are you."*

*"I can't. I mean— I've never done it willingly."*

*"Yes. You can. If you can hold the shift off when you want to, you can also welcome it when you want to. You've just never tried."*

*Corina walked back over to him, arms crossed. He was leaning against her door and pulling his boots off. "Come on. There's no one watching. I'll even turn my back if you want."*

*"Or," she smiled at him and opened the front door, "I can shuck my clothes in the comfort of my home."*

*He raised his brow, a grin spreading across his face.*

*While Liam remained on the porch, Corina paced around her small living room. The idea of shifting into her wolf willingly both thrilled and terrified her. There was so much she didn't know or understand about her own nature. Liam seemed willing to help, but what if he really had done something to her mother and this was all some elaborate ploy to get her to trust him?*

*She shook those thoughts from her head. One problem at a time. She could worry about Liam and his motives once she knew her mother was safe.*

*Liam was right. Corina could shift willingly. After she dropped her clothes on the sofa, she envisioned her wolf and was thrilled when the magic washed through her. She honestly wasn't sure why she'd never attempted such a thing before.*

*A minute later, she jumped through the small window from her bedroom to the grassy yard below. By standing on her hind legs, she was able to pull the pane down and secure it from the outside. A large black wolf was waiting for her when she made it to the front of the apartment and, within minutes, they were away from the building and safely hidden among the trees.*

*Like the night before, Liam hung back and let Corina lead the way. She was grace and beauty as she ran up the hill in the direction of her mother's inn. Shadows stretched out before them as the sun sank lower, but Corina knew these woods. Each fallen tree and running stream. Every rocky outcrop and blackberry bramble. She flew over the obstacles and Liam was right behind her the entire way. If she'd been on two legs, the hike would have taken over an hour, but on four, the pair made it in less than half the time.*

*Coming up behind the inn, Corina slowed and raised her muzzle to the evening air. She could still smell the hunters from the night before. Wary, she slowed even further. Liam seemed to sense her hesitancy and stopped next to her, nuzzling against her neck in reassurance.*

*A door banged shut around the front of the inn and Liam darted off in the direction of the noise. Corina wanted to call him back, but he was already gone.*

*The night air was broken by what sounded like a gunshot, followed by a long low whine that could only be Liam. Corina's heart began an erratic cadence.*

*Peaking around the corner of the building, her mind flew into a frenzy.*

*The beautiful black wolf lay on his side at the bottom of the inn's steps, a dart jutting from his hip. Kyle stood over him, rifle still pointed at the wolf. And next to him, rope in hand, stood Corina's mother.*

*"If he's here, Corina must be close," Bess said as she scanned the trees surrounding her property.*

*"If she is," Kyle replied, "we'll catch her."*

*Corina's heart thudded in her chest and she had to control the growl rising in her throat. What was Kyle talking about and why was her mother helping him? Had Kyle deliberately lied to Corina in order to lure her here? It was possible, but surely her mother wasn't in on it.*

*She had no idea what they were planning, but whatever it was, it didn't feel right. She needed to get Liam away from them until she could sort everything out.*

*Making a quick decision, Corina loped off down the hill to where she'd stashed her clothing the night before. Without the moon high in the sky, willing her body to shift back was easier than she expected. She donned her jeans and the bright red jacket, then jogged the short distance back to the inn.*

*Emerging from the woods, she watched in horror as her mother bent over the naked form of a now very human appearing, yet still very sedated, Liam. She was doing her best to bind his ankles and hands with the thick length of rope. Kyle was nowhere to be seen. Corina went cold.*

*She had to think fast. Could her mother really be doing this?*

*"Mom. Oh, thank god you're alright." She forced as much concern into her voice as she could. "Kyle scared me. He said he couldn't reach you. I got here as fast as I could."*

*She stopped short and plastered a confused expression on her face. "Is that Liam? What the hell are you doing?"*

*"Corina." Bess stood and turned to her daughter. "I'm sure this looks terrible. But he's dangerous."*

*"At the moment, he looks anything but dangerous. What happened to him?"*

*Her mother dropped her eyes, avoiding Corina's gaze entirely. "He attacked me, honey."*

*"Attacked you? Liam?"*

*Her mother gave her a stern look. She never did like being questioned. "Not all wolves are like you, Corina. You can't trust them."*

*"I didn't think you knew any other wolves."*

*Again, her mother dropped her gaze, refusing to look at Corina. "I don't. I mean, I just assume they aren't like you."*

*"Why don't you tell me what's really going on, Mom? Where's Kyle?"*

*Liam began to moan a little but still wasn't moving.*

*"I don't know what you're talking about." Bess lifted her chin, finally looking at her daughter. She took a hesitant step closer to Corina.*

*"I think you do. There's something you and Kyle aren't telling me." Corina backed toward the inn, wanting to keep her eyes on the forest. She cocked her head as her earlier conversation with Liam came to mind. "Who's my father, Mom?"*

*"I have no idea." Bess took another step toward Corina.*

*"You have no idea who you may have slept with that could pass the magic down to me? I find that fairly unsettling."*

*"I have no idea who your father is, just as I have no idea who your mother is," Bess hissed. Corina's legs went weak.*

*Was her mother actually saying that she wasn't her mother at all?*

*"I don't understand."*

*"I found you in the woods as a pup. Imagine my surprise when I took you in, fed you, and made a bed for you, and returned the next morning to find a human toddler where I left a wolf pup." Bess laughed, but it was devoid of any joy. "I called the sheriff on the spot, but he sent Kyle instead. He knew right away what you were and convinced me to keep you."*

*"There's money in werewolves," Kyle explained as he emerged from the side of the building. "I've been planning to bed you myself for years now, but Bess wouldn't have it. Said*

*you were too young, as if that matters. Then you moved out and it became harder to find a way." Corina was fairly certain she was going to be ill if he kept speaking. "Now, though? I'm glad I held off. We don't have to be concerned with half-breeds. As soon as this one showed up," he pointed to Liam, "Bess and I decided it was time to start cashing in on the secret."*

*All those hungry stares. He'd planned to do what he wanted whether she was willing or not. But certainly, there was no way to force Liam into this. "What are you talking about?"*

*"You may not feel it now," Kyle explained, "but the longer we keep you two together, you're bound to find comfort in each other. Between his impressive size and teeth, and your beautiful coat, the pups will fetch a pretty penny."*

*"You plan to breed me like a dog?" Corina really was going to vomit. She faced her mother. "And you agreed to this?"*

*Bess nodded.*

*"How could you?"*

*"Kyle can be very persuasive. Times are tight Corina. We need the money."*

*Liam moaned again and Corina thought he was trying to roll over. In his human form, however, he was still bound tightly.*

*Kyle still held the tranquilizer gun and Corina knew she needed to act swiftly or the next dart would be for her. He was closing in on her right, Bess on her left.*

*Corina raised her hands in surrender. "Just put the gun away. I'll do what you want." She looked toward the woman who'd raised her. "Just don't drug me."*

*"I knew you'd see reason. You've always done just what I wanted. It won't be so bad. Hell," Bess looked at the bound man behind her. "If I was a few years younger, I wouldn't mind being stuck with him."*

Corina managed a weak smile. "Mom, the gun." She glanced at Kyle, now just a few feet away.

"Put that thing away," Bess barked. "Corina's going to be a good girl."

Kyle looked dubious but knelt and placed the rifle on the ground at his feet. Bess took one more step forward and Corina burst from her position at the wall. The change ripped through her, shredding her jeans and jacket. Her muzzle was buried deep in Kyle's neck before he had time to register the movement. With a vicious shake of her head, his carotid artery opened and blood flew in an arc. Corina vaguely registered the sound of Bess's surprise before she was moving again.

In one graceful motion, Corina had the woman she'd always thought of as her mother pinned to the ground. A drop of Kyle's blood fell from the snarling muzzle of her wolf onto the terrified upturned face of the older woman. Bess opened her mouth to beg or command, Corina didn't care which. The words never came. A heartbeat later, Bess's throat matched that of Deputy Kyle Cobern.

Corina was trembling when she finally reached Liam's side. His grey eyes studied her blearily as she approached. It was an effort for Corina to focus and the shift took longer than she wanted, but eventually, she was able to use her human hands to loosen the ropes from his ankles and wrists. Corina helped him sit, then wrapped her arms around his neck and began to sob.

Still fighting the effects of the drug in his system, Liam's hands were clumsy as he reached around her and held her to his chest.

They sat like that, wrapped in each other's arms, for several long minutes before Corina inhaled-a deep lungful of air and wiped her eyes. Together they gathered their shredded remnants of clothing and went inside to wash up before calling the authorities about the animal attack outside.

*Once everything was in order at The Den, and Bess had been laid to rest, the pair locked the doors of The Den and began the quest that would bring them even closer together. Somewhere, a pair of wolves had lost their daughter. With Liam's help, Corina intended to find them.*

Doria was wide awake as she finished reading. Was this her new favorite short story? No. Did she hate it? Also no. Perhaps Miles was better at figuring her out than she'd given him credit for.

Flipping through the book, Doria found two other stories that she also didn't hate, but none that she liked quite as much as *Seeing Red*. It was the wee hours of the morning when she finally snapped the cover shut and drifted off into a peaceful slumber.

Sometime in the night, she dreamt of Miles. He was a hunter. Doria was his prey.

# 7

AS EXPECTED, the women got off to a slow start the following day. Felicity grumbled as she staggered, bleary-eyed, into the small kitchen and accepted the cup of coffee in Doria's outstretched hand.

"You look about as tired as I feel," Felicity said as she blew steam over the rim of the mug.

"I was up late last night reading."

"More psychopathic killers and blood-covered clowns?" Felicity raised an eyebrow at her friend. Doria's roommate wasn't herself much of a reader, but she was fascinated by the bloody books Doria seemed to favor.

"No actually. I read another one that Miles gave me."

"Oh? Do tell!" She sat on the couch, feet up and snuggling her mug to her chest.

"Well. I have to admit it was better than the first, but still a little on the swoony side. There were at least a few beasts and badasses in this one, so a step up for sure." Doria stretched her neck and sighed. "Anyway, it was enough to keep me interested, at least."

"And when are you taking it back to discuss with the sexy book nerd?" Felicity asked with a grin.

"Tonight I suppose."

"Why not now?"

"Because, unless you forgot, we have plans, remember?"

"Well, we never made official plans, and I think even if we did, they are now changing. I want. . . No, I *need* to see this hottie for myself." Felicity had bounced up and was pulling Doria to her feet. "Get dressed. We're going book shopping."

As they walked toward the downtown area, the sun cast dappled patterns through the trees. The walkway under their feet was patterned in the pixilated shapes of leaves. Several birds sang in the trees.

"So tell me more about this guy. I want to know what to expect when we get there," Felicity prompted.

"I don't really know what to say. I told you before, he isn't my type. And to be fair, the first time we talked I thought he was kind of an ass." Her voice was tinged with uncertainty. "But, then we had a nice time last night. It's just weird. I forget the buttoned-up shirts and the neatly trimmed hair. He's different, but in a good way."

"You should try to see what's *under* the buttoned-up shirts. Then you might be sold." Felicity bumped her with her shoulder and they continued walking passed the grungy bar and to the clothing consignment next door to Vespertine Books.

There were more people out and enjoying the milder spring weather and, while the sidewalks weren't crowded, they certainly weren't abandoned either. As Doria and Felicity approached the spot between the clothing shop and the dry cleaners, where the little bookshop should have been, they found only a blank brick wall, colorfully tagged with graffiti. The worn wooden sign was missing and so was the glass-paned door to the shop.

Doria's stomach churned with agitation. She was certain this was the spot. Had her memory been playing tricks on her?

Remembering the trouble she'd had the night before, she walked the length of the block, Felicity at her side, scanning each business and door they crossed.

"Are you sure you've got the right street?" Felicity asked gently, a tinge of disappointment lacing the words.

"Yes, I *was* sure," Doria frowned, "Now, I don't know. I just could have sworn this was the spot. Obviously, I was wrong. "

"Hey, it's alright," Felicity reassured her friend, placing a comforting hand on Doria's shoulder. "It was a late night for both of us. We're probably just sleep deprived and got turned around somewhere. Let's grab a burger and then we can try again."

Doria nodded, the tension leaving her shoulders as she leaned into Felicity. Something wasn't right, but she wouldn't let it spoil the afternoon. She could examine it later.

Heading toward the crosswalk, however, she looked back over her shoulder. Leaning up against the brick-and-mortar wall, she saw the figure of a man. It took a minute for her mind to register where she'd seen him before. It was the odd guy, Peter Smith, whom she'd met her first night in the shop. He probably knew where the actual store was located. Their eyes locked for a moment, but when Doria opened her mouth to call out to him and ask, he put his head down and turned away, heading in the opposite direction up the street. Within moments, he was lost to the thin crowd.

Felicity tugged on her sleeve as the light changed and Doria hurried to cross with the other pedestrians.

Her stomach grumbled and she laughed, knowing a fat greasy burger was just what she needed to get her head on straight.

The moon stood sentinel in the sky, a pale witness to Doria's resolve as she retraced her steps through the streets. Her heart pounded in her chest, heavy with both anticipation and trepidation. After lunch, the women had looked up and down a couple of the side streets, but the mysterious bookshop remained elusive. Felicity brushed it off with a laugh and announced that she needed to get home to ready herself for another date with her newest conquest.

After she'd left, Doria grabbed her satchel and the book she'd borrowed and set out to prove to herself that she was not, in fact, losing her mind.

She turned the corner onto the street where the bar and dry cleaners sat, and expected nothing but disappointment, but when she reached the space between the shops, there it was—the weathered sign emerging from the shadows like a specter in the night. The sight of it relieved her, but the feeling was quickly chased by a deep unsettling. How could it have been missing earlier in the day?

"Get a fucking grip, Doria," she muttered to herself. She took a deep breath and put her palm on the frame of the door. As she pushed it open, the familiar smell of ink and paper, leather and canvas, enveloped her. She stepped inside, welcoming the balm it had on her frayed nerves.

"Ah, Doria James," Miles greeted her from behind the counter as he slipped the thick glasses from his face. "I'm so pleased you've returned." His voice was smooth and honey rich and she felt a thrill run through her at the sound of it.

As much as she could stand there and listen to him say her name all night, there was something else she needed him to explain. "Where did the shop go earlier?" she demanded, her dark eyes narrowing at him.

"I'm not sure I know," he answered cryptically.

"Not sure you know? So it did disappear?"

"No," he drew the word out. "It's always here."

"But it wasn't *here*." This entire conversation was completely insane. Shops didn't just up and vanish, only to return several hours later.

"I can assure you it was. Perhaps you just missed it?" He had actual amusement in his eyes now. It only served to make her angry.

"This isn't funny Miles."

"I never said it was." His face lost the merriment it had contained. He reached a hand up and rubbed the back of his neck, studying the ceiling above him. "Sometimes this place has a mind of its own. It's all I can say."

"Right," Doria scoffed, her skepticism plain. "If you don't want to discuss it, fine. I guess I won't come looking for you again."

His eyes snapped to her and something like fear flashed across his features. "No. You've got to come back." The words were barely more than a breathy exhale.

"Not if I can't find it!" She reached into her bag and pulled out the book he'd given her. "Here you go. I appreciate you lending it to me." She laid it on the counter and turned to leave.

"You can't go. Not yet." He stepped around to the front of the counter and reached out as if he'd touch her. At the last moment, he pulled his hand back and shook his head. He smiled broadly. "You have to tell me what you thought of it first."

"Seriously?" She asked.

"Seriously." He nodded.

Doria closed her eyes and blew out a breath, cocking her head down as she decided something. "I liked it more than the first one."

"I thought you might. Did you read the third entry?" Miles prompted, leaning forward in interest.

"Yep. And a couple of the others."

"And?"

Doria realized she wasn't going to be getting out of the shop anytime soon. Removing her jacket and placing her bag on the counter, she walked over and sank into what was becoming her favorite chair.

"It was. . .better. Still not my favorite, but at least I felt a decent connection to the modern setting and to Corina. She was way closer to the strong female protagonists I like. Plus, anytime there's throats being ripped out. . . let's just say I'm one of those people who believe the ending can save the whole story if it's done right."

"Now we might be getting somewhere," he smiled.

"Also, I didn't feel like I was reading porn, so there's that."

"You're very judgmental when it comes to the typical romance tropes." He said it with a grin, but Doria still felt herself grimace. Was she being judgy? Maybe, but that hadn't really ever been her intention.

"Yikes. You might be right." She chewed on her bottom lip.

"Don't worry. I'm not so easily offended when it comes to my reading habits. I read what I like and I have learned that it really doesn't matter what others think of my book choices. I'm happy you found that one a little more appealing, but I'd be lying if I said it was my favorite."

Doria realized she hadn't ever really asked him what his favorite genre was. He'd given her his list of favorite books, but they were all over the map—some classics, some epic fantasy, even a few historical fiction and mysteries thrown in. "I haven't asked. If you had to read just one genre for the rest of your life, what would it be?"

His face stilled and he drew a small sharp breath, then seemed to shake off whatever had made him pause and gave a little chuckle. "I can't imagine being stuck with only one choice for all eternity."

"I didn't say all eternity, I said for the rest of your life."

He shrugged. "Semantics."

"Oh come on! What do you like to read the most then?" She laughed at his refusal of such a simple question when she'd been so sure of her own answer to the same question only days before. It was amazing really. Doria had laughed more in this man's presence than she had in the last few years with anyone, save for Felicity.

"Fine. If I had to choose, I'd say true fantasy. Fairies and dark forests. Ogres, orcs, and magic that seeps into your bones and doesn't let go until you're stuck with the most delicious sort of book hangover. Add in a few sultry bits and spicy scenes and it's the perfect book. As long as the storytelling is good, of course. I have read a few piles of manure over the years." His eyes gleamed with mischief as if he knew Doria never expected that particular answer.

Her cheeks flushed as she looked at him, sure he was being insincere. "You're joking, right?"

"Am I?" Miles challenged, his voice low and intimate, a conspiratorial smile tugging at the corner of his mouth.

Doria's pulse quickened. "I'm not so sure," she replied coyly. Even if he was being less than truthful, the allure of him saying he was into the romantasy stuff made her stomach flip in odd little swoops, if for no other reason than it was just so unexpected.

"I've always believed there's more to stories than meets the eye," he mused, breaking the brief but charged silence. "Sometimes, they reveal truths we never knew we were seeking."

"Or. . . maybe they just distract us from reality," Doria countered, attempting to regain her composure.

"Either way, I believe it's your turn to pick a story for me to read." He gestured at the towering shelves surrounding them.

"You want me to choose a book for you?" She looked at him from the corner of her eye.

He nodded. "And one for yourself. Then we can discuss them both next time I see you and decide once and for all if we can ever bridge the book snob gap between us."

She snorted a laugh but was already moving toward the shelves. It was a simple game and she could play it just as well as Miles, but a small part of her really didn't want to disappoint him with whatever selection she made. She shoved the thought aside and headed toward the back where she'd seen a collection of monster stories, hoping she could find something creepy and scary to discuss with the shop owner. She would embrace the challenge and the power of the story. Authors she knew placed a certain amount of trust in their readers. They were sharing the gift of their words. Similarly, the reader trusted the author not to let them down. She just hoped she could find a book that wouldn't betray that trust.

It didn't take her long to scan the shelves. There were volumes of werewolves, vampires, zombies, and creatures from the deep. Outer space viruses and demonic clowns. She skimmed past skin walkers, lunatic gods, and possessed dolls until her eyes fell on a pair of blood-red covers with the deepest black lettering on the spines. A set of devil horns crowned the titles and Doria was immediately drawn to the copies. Miles had said to grab two books, he never said she couldn't pick the same book for both of them. She'd never read this one, but if she could judge a book by its cover, it was going to prove to be amazing.

Returning to where Miles sat, long legs stretched out before him, she smiled broadly.

He looked to her hands and frowned.

"You never said we had to read different books."

"Yes, but. . . "his face broke into a wide grin. "You've never read that one?"

"Nope." Her smile faltered. "Wait. Have you?"

"Doesn't matter. You chose it. I'll read it again." He stood and held out his hand to her.

Doria stepped into his space. As she transferred the book to his hand, heat from him radiated to her fingertips. She felt it all the way in her toes. Heart beating wildly, she inhaled the masculine scent of him. It was leather and sandalwood and oh-so-delicious.

Miles leaned down and placed his lips near her ear. "Enjoy the story, Doria James." It was a whisper and promise all rolled into one.

Caught up in the moment, she tilted her head up to capture his lips with her own, but he pulled back ever so slightly. His eyes were alight with fire but also a gentle insistence. "Read the book first, then come back and we can. . ." his voice trailed off with an unspoken promise.

Doria's cheeks flushed, but she refused to let him get the better of her. "And what if I decide not to?"

"Let's just call it optimism." He looked down into her upturned face.

She nodded and clutched the book to her chest like a shield before reaching for her things.

Back straight and refusing to look back at Miles, she made her way to the exit.

"Goodnight Doria," his voice lingered in the air behind her. "See you soon."

Doria took her time walking the distance back to her apartment. As much as she was eager to dive into a book of demons and devils, she wanted to process the storm of thoughts tumbling through her head.

The night air caressed her face, and if she wasn't such a practical person, she would have described the feeling as magical. It sent a shiver down her spine. She still couldn't explain the loss of the shop earlier in the day, nor could she reconcile how much smaller it seemed from the outside. It had a feeling of otherworldliness every time she crossed the threshold. Add in the fact that no other patrons, with the exceptions of Cassie and Peter, had ever been there while Doria was visiting and the feeling that she got from Miles himself, and it added up to a whole pot of strange. Either the shop itself had some sort of spell cast over it, or she did.

But this was life, not a story. There had to be some other explanation. Doria would find the answer, even if it meant breaking the enchantment she found in Miles.

Doria sat alone in her dimly lit room, the velvety darkness outside pressing against her window. She held a thin book bound in lavender leather, its pages worn and delicate, like the petals of a long-forgotten flower. It wasn't the book she'd chosen for herself. Miles must have slipped it into her bag without her noticing.

As she began to read, her cheeks flushed with color and her breath quickened. The story of the fae prince and his human consort was far more explicit than she had expected.

With each turn of the page, the words became sultrier and steamier. If she looked at the online reviews, at least four little chili peppers would be included in the postings. Swirling tongues and sharpened teeth. Driving need. Thrusting and suckling. Creamy skin and satin pleasure. She tried to focus on the words for the sake of the story, but her thoughts kept drifting back to Miles, his mischievous smile and those deep-knowing eyes. By giving her this book, it felt as though he'd handed her a secret key, an invitation to explore the depths of their desire for one another. The sensation both excited and frightened her.

She finished the book in record time and then tossed it at her feet in the bed. Her mind was racing with desire and doubt. Throwing caution to the wind, she rose from the tangled mess of sheets and ventured out into the night.

The streets were deserted, the world wrapped in a cloak of shadows. As Doria approached the bookshop, worry nagged at her that she'd find it once again missing. The sign wasn't visible in the deep gloom. A noise from across the street startled her. Her heart thudded in her chest. She looked around but saw no one. When she turned back, the worn wooden sign was just where it should be.

It was late and the shop should have been closed, but when she turned the knob, it yielded silently.

To her surprise, flickering candlelight cast dancing patterns on the walls. Miles shouldn't have had any candles within the space. One wrong move and the shelves of dry parchment would go up in a flash.

She stepped further in, not wanting to call out just yet. As she approached the counter, her eyes fell on an open bottle of wine and two glasses. She thought about running. The last thing she wanted was to walk in on Miles with another woman. That thought, and all others, left her head as she stepped closer to the sitting area.

Miles was there, reclining on a plush sofa. He looked so different from how she'd remembered him before. His tailored shirt had been discarded, leaving him clad only in jeans and his thick black glasses—a book tented on his chest. Shadows obscured his trunk and arms, but her imagination filled in the gaps well enough. His gaze swept over her and a slow easy smile crept over his face. He removed his glasses, setting them on the table in a deliberate motion. How could removing your glasses be so sexy? It was like a mini-strip show, just for her. He stretched out his long legs and pulled his hands up behind his head. As his arms escaped the shadows, Doria caught sight of something unexpected—a full sleeve of tattoos decorating his left arm. The pattern was an intricate script. She couldn't make out the words from this distance, but she could see the elegant swirls that accompanied the font. It suited him perfectly.

"Couldn't sleep?" he asked, his voice low and rich. A shiver ran down her spine and she found herself unable to tear her eyes away from the tattoos and the bare expanse of flesh across his muscled chest. Miles had definitely been hiding out under all the starched collars and fitted vests he wore.

"No," she admitted, feeling suddenly shy in his presence. "I couldn't stop thinking about. . . the book."

"Ah, yes." The knowing smile on his face made her shiver even more. "It tends to have that effect on people."

Doria was hesitant but needed some answers. "Did you give it to me for a reason?"

"Perhaps," he replied as his eyes locked on hers. "Or perhaps I simply wanted to see what you'd think of it."

Doria's heart raced, her curiosity about the shop and her desire warring within her. She knew the magnetic pull she felt toward Miles couldn't be real, but she refused to believe there was something magical lurking beneath the surface of their connection.

"Tell me the truth Miles, is this real?" Her voice was trembling slightly.

"Is what real, Doria James?"

"You. This shop. All of it. Is it real or only a magic spell?"

Miles' expression shifted, becoming serious as he regarded her. "It's real. I can assure you. But magic is a complex thing. Sometimes it's woven into the very fabric of our lives, guiding us toward moments of discovery and transformation. What some would say is an enchantment, others would call a curse."

"And this? Is this a curse?" She asked, her breath catching in her throat as she gazed at him and his perfectly sculpted arms and torso. Her world narrowed down to the space between them.

"This is certainly not a curse," he murmured. For a fraction of a moment, they were suspended in time, the air between them crackling with possibility.

Doria held the smutty book in trembling hands, the weight of what could come next pressing down on her. She glanced at Miles, his tattoos unreadable even as she closed the distance between them. Her breath was ragged as she handed him back the book, hoping he'd brush her fingers with his own once again. The need to feel the little thrill of connection between them was a palpable, growing thing.

Her voice was a breathy whisper as she said, "Thank you for lending me this one."

He lifted an eyebrow. "Are you saying you enjoyed it?"

"I did," she admitted, heat flooding her cheeks.

"Is that so?" He set the book down behind him and turned back to her. The scent of musty books and the aroma of heady wine mingled, giving the air an aura of forbidden pleasure. "And what exactly did you like about it?"

"That you gave it to me."

"So you were thinking of me while you read it?" His eyes held fire and she wanted nothing more than to burn in the depths of it.

Biting her lower lip, she held his gaze and nodded.

Miles reached up and tucked a lock of hair behind her ear. "I was hoping you'd say that." He drew the back of his knuckles down her cheek, to her neck, and then across her collarbone. His eyes roamed over her and she felt need pooling in her breasts and lower into her belly.

Miles leaned in and brushed his lips across hers, feather-light. Doria groaned. "I like that sound, Doria James. But unfortunately for me, it's time you woke up."

Doria's brow furrowed.

"Doria, wake up."

Miles' voice had risen in pitch and sounded an awful lot like. . . Felicity.

"Come on lazy bones," Felicity said. "You're going to be late for work."

Doria groaned as the sunlight in her apartment danced across her retinas and she blinked.

"I don't know what—or who—you were dreaming about, Peaches. But based on the sounds you were making, I'm gonna say it was a good one." Felicity laughed as she handed a mug of piping hot coffee to her friend and danced out of the room.

# 8

**DORIA** couldn't believe she'd fallen asleep before even cracking the book she'd chosen to read with Miles. Now she was late for work and had intended to swing by the library at lunch to chat with Cassondra. She was hoping the librarian would be able to shed a little light on the shop and the curious feeling she'd had about it. She had also hoped to visit Miles that evening, but what would he think if she showed up without having finished her reading assignment? Then she'd have to admit to stopping by just for the sake of seeing him. And after that dream, she wanted to see *all* of him.

She made the most of her messy hair by piling it high in a knot on the top of her head and swiped on some smudgy eyeliner. She shoved the red and black book into her bag, put on her sensible shoes, and headed for another long day.

The morning rush wasn't as bad as she'd expected and she was able to head to the library during her mid-shift break. She could have used the time to read the story she had, but something told her talking to the librarian might be a better use of her time.

She checked in at the information table and was told Cassondra was in the back of the stacks at one of the references tables. Walking through the brightly lit space and listening to the patrons speaking in hushed tones brought a wave of nostalgia to Doria. She mentally kicked herself for giving up on school, all for some guy who looked good in a pair of snug jeans. This could have been her life if she'd been thinking with her head instead of her heart.

"Doria," Cassondra greeted as she made her way past the banks of computers and reading tables. "What a splendid surprise!"

"Hello Cassondra," then quickly amended when the pixie-haired woman scowled at her, "Cassie."

"Did you come round so I could show off the library to you?"

"Yes and no. I haven't got time for a full tour today, I'm due back to work in just a bit. But there was something else I was hoping you could help me with."

Doria proceeded to tell Cassie about the strange feelings she had about the bookshop and her hopes that, since the librarian was one of the only people she'd ever seen inside it, she might help her understand what was going on.

Cassie nodded but didn't interrupt as she listened to Doria. When the younger woman had finished, she looked hopefully at the librarian.

Cassondra tapped a pencil on her desk as she thought about how to respond.

"It's true. I do spend a good amount of time in the shop, although not as much as I used to. I have a connection with Miles, as I'm sure you are aware, but it's not quite the same as the one you seem to be forming with him."

"So, do you think there's something odd about the place?" Doria asked.

"It's a little more than odd." Cassie sighed heavily. "I wish I could explain to you what I know, but unfortunately it just isn't the kind of thing to do quickly."

"Why not?" Doria almost yelled the words, then remembered where she was and looked around sheepishly in apology.

"It's not how the story is supposed to go. It needs to unfold slowly for you to fully grasp it all."

"What does that mean? What story?"

"His story. My – Miles. Miles' story is a complex one." The dark-haired beauty took in the frown on Doria's face and added. "I can't tell you what you need to know right now, but I might be able to show you. This library is filled with some rather interesting things. Follow me."

Doria was frustrated but could do nothing other than follow along in Cassie's wake. They navigated several towering stacks and finally came to the history section. There were the usual books on war, politics, monarchies, and innovations. Doria even saw a small collection on medical history and another on ancient trade and industrialization. Cassie passed these by and finally came to a single shelf containing the history of the small town they lived in. There were several about the local governance, interesting historical facts, popular tourist spots to visit, and one or two that seemed to contain records and articles about local businesses and landmarks. These books looked a little used and faded, but Cassie pointed to one in particular and suggested Doria might enjoy it. On closer inspection, Doria realized it was a moderately sized volume on the history and folklore of the town.

"I know you don't have time to sit and read through it here but check it out and take it with you. I'm hopeful it will set you on the right track."

Doria was still confused, but anything was better than what she'd come with.

"Do you mind if I ask you one more thing?" Cassie was just scanning the barcode of the folklore book into her computer.

"Sure." She looked up from the desk. "Hopefully I'll even be able to answer it this time."

Doria's lips quirked into a half smile.

"You mentioned a woman named Elenor the other day. Miles said she's a bit of a folklore legend in town."

"That's putting it mildly," Cassie replied.

"Well, do you suppose, she might be able to help me figure things out?"

Cassie thought for a minute, chewing on her lower lip as she did so. "It's possible, she could give you some answers. She's always been very fond of Miles. Tell you what. Read up on that book a bit, and then we can plan to get together tomorrow night if Elenor is willing."

"That sounds like a plan. If it's fine with you both, I'd like to bring my friend Felicity as well." Doria grabbed her phone. "What's your number? I'll text you mine."

As she hurried back to work, she was filled with new vigor.

The late lunch and early evening crowds at the café were relatively light and Doria was absolutely thrilled when her relief server came in a few minutes early. The day hadn't yet made way to evening and the wind wasn't too vicious. Doria decided, instead of going home, she'd head to the small park across from the café and dive into the book she'd chosen the night before.

Felicity stopped in just as she was leaving. "Whatcha up to?"

"Quite a bit actually, if you can believe it."

Doria gave her friend a rundown on the conversation she'd had with Cassondra and the plan to do a little research into her very own mystery man. She explained the plan to meet with Elenor the next day.

"Hey, would you want to come with? I could probably use your help."

"Absolutely! Just call me Daphne and point me to the mystery machine and Scooby snacks!"

"OK, well, that would make me either Velma or Shaggy," Doria held up her hand in a stop gesture, "so I'm gonna stop you right there."

"Fair enough. But why wait til tomorrow? We could head over there now if you want."

"Cassondra wanted to check with Elenor first to make sure it's cool for us to come by. And I really was hoping to see Miles tonight."

Felicity waggled her copper brows. "You gonna tell him about the dream I interrupted this morning?"

Doria's face flushed with the thought. That was one dream she hoped she'd never forget. "Umm. . . that would be a hard no. I'm not telling him."

"So it was about Miles then? I knew it!"

"You got me. Now scoot. I'm heading to the park to read for few before I head to the shop."

Felicity was rummaging around in her enormous purse as she answered. "You got it. But first, I have a gift for you."

"A gift?" Doria looked at her skeptically. "Why do I have a feeling I'm not going to like this *gift?*"

"Always so cynical, Peaches." Felicity handed her a tiny gift bag, a wicked smile on her face. "I'll see you later tonight." Doria peeked inside. She cringed when she saw the square foil condom packets arranged within.

Felicity didn't need to say more. She waved as she walked to her small beat-up car parked on the street in front of the café.

The park was relatively uninhabited, save for a few mothers and their small children running amuck. She watched as an older child flew a kite. The sight of the bright rainbow fish soaring high above made Doria smile.

She found a bench along the grassy expanse and settled in.

Unfortunately, Doria realized as she cracked the black and red beauty open, she hadn't chosen a specific story for them to read. Knowing Miles had probably read them all, she just went for the first in the book. If it was as dark and mysterious as the cover implied, it was bound to be good. Demons and devils. What more could she ask for?

## The Princess and the Promise

*Power, trust, betrayal—these are the forces that have shaped our fate.*

*Mila wasn't sure if she had ever been so miserable in her life. Cold, wet, and out of options, she stood outside the castle gate and told herself this was a good idea. It would work. It had to work.*

*When she threw her hood back and called to the guards, she ignored the freezing pellets of rain as they stung her skin. She ignored the sniggers and laughter as she was escorted from the gate to the castle's entrance. She ignored the hostile looks and the turned backs as she made her way to the throne room. Most of all, she ignored the thundering of her heart as she knelt before the king and queen of Thornscarp and asked for a marriage alliance with their son, the brutal Prince Gregor.*

Marriage alliance? Dear god no. Please don't let this be a romance in disguise.

At least a brutal prince sounded promising.


*"And why is it you come to us, child, and not your noble father?" The King asked, a laugh playing at the corners of his flinty mouth.*

*Guards stood to either side of the thrones. On the left was a woman with scaled skin the color of moss and golden feathers flowing from her head in a long cascade down her back. A long scar ran from one of her lavender eyes, across the bridge of her nose and into the neck of her armor. On the right stood the biggest man Mila had ever seen. He towered above the king and queen. Who makes his armor? Mila thought. His face was both human and not unattractive. Large bull horns grew from his temples and his lower legs were those of some mighty beast— complete with cloven hooves rather than feet. Both guards stared straight ahead, blank unfeeling expressions on their faces.*

*"He was unable, Your Grace." Mila kept her eyes downcast and spoke with a calm she did not feel.*

*"Unable or unwilling?" he replied.*

*There was no good way to answer, but Mila felt the truth was required. "Both," she said simply.*

*"And you take this responsibility on yourself?" The queen asked. Mila ventured a glance toward the woman then immediately regretted it. If the king was fearsome to look at, the queen was downright brutal. Long twisted horns sat over a face that was at once stunning and cruel. Her long auburn hair was braided to her waist, and she wore a leather breastplate scarred by countless slashes.*

*The queen was not someone to be tangled with.*

*"I am, Your Grace."*

*"And why is it, child, you think we should even consider this offer?" The question was fair enough, but Mila still felt the tone of disapproval from the warrior queen. She knew what the queen was thinking. How could a simple woman from Gildernosh ever be enough for a warrior prince of Thornscarp?*

*All the lands knew the royal family of Thornscarp had deemed it time for Prince Gregor to find a bride. It was their plan to create a solid alliance with one of the wealthy neighboring kingdoms and, while Mila's own kingdom had wealth to spare, it had also been under constant siege from its neighbors to the west. Kingdoms of brute strength looking to take Gildernosh and its fruitful gem mines by force rather than political alliance. Mila, knowing the risks, had suggested to her father an alliance with Thornscarp. Her face still stung from the slap he'd given her and from the shame of being thrown out of his presence. The beautiful people of Gildernosh would never debase themselves by forming an alliance with the demon beasts of Thornscarp. No matter the cost to the kingdom or its people.*

Demon beasts. Doria could work with demon beasts.

*But Mila loved her people and she loved her home. She would sacrifice for them by sealing an alliance with a Prince who could rally his troops to defend her homeland. In time, her people would come to accept the price that needed to be paid for their safety and their freedom. She only hoped her father would understand.*

*It had taken her no more than a day to decide. In the dead of night, while the beautiful people of Gildernosh slept in their comfortable beds, Mila saddled her horse and set out for the border with Thornscarp.*

*"Your Grace," Mila began. "Gildernosh may not have armies as vast and as trained as yours, but we can offer wealth enough to supply your soldiers with any and all weaponry needed. Our people are hard-working and our harvests are plentiful. We may supply your people with food enough to ensure not a soul goes hungry. Add in our harbors on the east and access to the seas will be at your disposal. In exchange, I only seek your assistance in sending a message to those who would seek to invade our lands and take these things– which I offer you freely– by force."*

*The queen tilted her chin down, not in a nod of agreement, but in contemplation. Mila's heart sank as the queen's eyes lit up and a smirk stretched her full lips.*

*"You've shown bravery coming here, and for that I commend you. Stay with us the week and we shall see if you are truly a worthy bride for my son."*

*Mila released the breath she'd been holding. A week in the castle was easy enough. If she truly meant to wed Prince Gregor, she would be spending more time than that in the company of the brutal family. "You do me a great honor," she said.*

*"Thak," the queen barked. "Take the princess to the blue room. I trust you to see that she is comfortable during her stay." The large horned guard stepped forward and dipped toward the queen in a bow.*

*"Yes, Your Grace." His voice was deep and rich. Mila stepped after him but turned at the last moment.*

*"I beg your pardon; might I at least meet Prince Gregor."*

*The queens' face was unreadable. "Of course, child. I'll see that you get introduced this evening."*

*The guard walked several paces ahead of Mila as they made their way out of the throne room and to a grand stone staircase leading up into the castle. Mila once again found herself attempting to ignore the frosty looks and whispered insults as she passed servants, courtiers, and soldiers who seemed to occupy every room and passageway of the castle. Her escort took no notice of the others as he led her silently through the stone walkways. His legs were considerably longer than Mila's, but he seemed to take care in matching his pace to hers.*

*When they reached a solid wooden door at the end of a long hallway several floors above the throne room, the guard stopped and dipped his head toward her.*

*"Thak, is it?" Mila asked. He nodded once more. "May I use your given name, or do you prefer something else?"*

*"Thak is fine, Your Highness." He stood next to the door, legs slightly parted and hands behind his back.*

*She smiled. "Oh, we can't have me using a familiar name and you sticking with Your Highness. Please call me Mila."*

*"I'm afraid the queen would not approve," the guard answered.*

*Mila sighed. "Very well. This is my room then?"*

*He nodded brusquely and pushed the door open, dipping his head to avoid hitting his impressive horns on the jam, as he stepped in before her. Mila followed and took it all in. The room was clean and tidy, if sparsely furnished. A large stone fireplace occupied one wall and a simple oak framed bed sat against the other. A thick piled mattress and a sea of lush comforters nearly buried the bed frame. Matching velvet drapes covered the windows and blue sconces covered the lamps on both the table and affixed to the walls.*

"There's a washroom through there," Thak pointed to a door in the corner between the bed and the windows. "It gets cold in the night. I'll light your hearth before you retire."

Mila turned and took it all in. "I've left my horse in the stable along with my bag. If you'd be kind enough to show me the way, I'd like to tend to her and retrieve my things."

Mila noted a slight widening of the guard's eyes. They were a deep rich brown, nearly the same shade as the hair covering his lower legs.

"Is that a problem?" She asked.

"Not at all. I assumed you'd like a servant to fetch your belongings."

"I need to learn my way around if I'm to be a guest in the castle. There's no sense in having someone else tend what I can easily do myself."

"Of course, Your Highness."

Thak escorted her back down the stairs, but rather than exiting from the door Mila had come through earlier in the day, he took them around through the kitchen and out a side door to the stables. Mila was shown to her horse. She spent nearly an hour brushing the stallion and whispering in its ear as she fed it carrots from a bucket by the tack room.

Thak stood silently by the entrance while she tended to the animal and retrieved her belongings. When she was ready to return to her room, the guard attempted to take her bags, but she refused. "Again, there is no sense in having you labor when I can easily handle my own luggage."

When they reached the door to the blue room, Thak pushed it open but did not step inside. "Water should have been drawn for your bath. Dinner is in an hour. I'll be out here when you're ready to go down."

"Thank you," Mila said as she stepped past him and shut the door behind her.

*It took all of Mila's strength not to break into tears as the door thudded shut. She knew the citizens of Thornscarp were part demon warriors and had heard tales of the differences among them. She'd even met a few in the past at functions at home, but those had looked almost completely human to her. She hadn't properly prepared herself for the scars and horns, scales and teeth of them.*

*She'd never even seen a likeness of Prince Gregor. All she knew was that he was fierce and courageous in battle. He had a deadly reputation but she knew nothing of the man himself. What if he was covered in plates or fur? What if he had his mother's horns and the teeth of a viper? What if she could never love him or even like him? Worse, what if she feared him?*

*All the possibilities roiled around in her head and in her gut, but none of them were going to be answered now. Best to put on a brave face until she knew for certain what she'd just offered of herself. And who knew, perhaps the royal family or the prince himself would reject her offer by the end of the week. Then she'd be right back where she'd started.*

*Mila walked through the chamber, pulling her braid loose.*

*Thak was right. As she entered the small bathing chamber and pulled her dress off, she was relieved to see steam rising from the deep tub in the center of the space. She hadn't seen warm water in what felt like ages and her muscles ached at the mere sight of it. Kicking off her boots and shedding the last of her clothing, she sighed and then stepped into the blissful warmth.*

*By the time the water had cooled, her fingers were wrinkled and her head was calmer. She didn't know why the thick, soft towel at the tub's side surprised her so much. Surely even the mightiest of royal families needed a good bath on occasion.*

*She dragged her fingers through her long honey-hued hair, then retrieved the only decent gown she'd been able to fit in her pack. It was slightly crumpled but would have to do. The deep rust color set nicely against her ivory skin. She only hoped it would be enough to win at least a glance from the prince.*

*Thak, true to his word, was waiting patiently right outside her door when she opened it. "Oh, I hope you aren't going to be stuck standing out here all week on my account."*

*There it was again, the slight widening of his eyes when she spoke. There and then gone in a blink.*

*"Your Highness." He nodded. "This way please."*

*When he led her through the castle this time, they went back toward the throne room and the main halls. Mila could hear music drifting from up ahead and the air took on the wonderful aroma of roasted meat. Her stomach made a loud rumbling noise and she grimaced. "Sorry," she directed at the guard when he glanced over his shoulder at her. "It's been a long day and I haven't eaten much."*

*"You should have said something." He turned his head forward and Mila wondered how difficult it was to navigate the halls without hitting his impressive horns on the archways. "The queen will be displeased if her guest is not treated with hospitality."*

*"No. You've all been. . . lovely." Mila cleared her throat and continued on behind him.*

*The doors of the great hall were thrown wide— music and laughter flowed out as they approached. Thak stepped back to allow Mila to enter ahead of him and the noise dulled almost instantly. Heads turned her way and she was greeted with a volley of sneers, smirks, and whispers. Mila lifted her chin and walked between the tables until she stood before the king and queen. Seated to the queen's right was an achingly beautiful man not much older than she was herself. Mila dipped into a curtsy and did not rise until the queen spoke.*

*"Ah child. You've made it."* There was coldness in her eyes and in her voice. She rose with a warrior's grace, as did the gorgeous young man at her side. *"May I present to you my son, the Prince of Thronscarp."*

The impact of the queen's words left Mila temporarily immobilized. It was only when Thak stepped up and bowed to the royals that she realized how foolish she probably looked. She turned to the prince and dipped her head in his direction. *"Your Highness."*

Gregor studied her for a moment, then with an exceedingly bored look on his face, turned his attention to the soldier seated beside him.

Color flooded Mila's cheeks, but she held her head high and smiled to the king and queen. Thak extended an arm, directing her to a neighboring table with two empty seats. She gratefully sank into her chair and was pleased when Thak took the other. At least she wouldn't be alone with a group of soldiers and courtiers who likely would rather see her starve than offer her cordial dinner conversation.

The surrounding chairs were occupied by three other men and a young woman who all appeared to be related. Two of the men and the woman all had silvery white hair and upturned noses. They also had bright green eyes with elliptical pupils running vertically through the centers. The third man had the same cat-like eyes but was completely bald. Not a single frosty hair on his head. His ears held a series of looping gold rings up either side. Mila noted how the others at the table had left ample room for the big guard and his impressive horns. He nodded to the others and dipped his chin toward Mila. *"Princess Mila of Gildernosh. Your Highness, this is Ograt, Nox, Ram, and Petra."* He pointed to each in turn.

The bald man, Ograt, smiled broadly and raised his cup toward her. "A pleasure to make your acquaintance."

As if his words were a signal, the other three also turned in their chairs and raised their cups. Mila smiled in return. "Thank you. It's nice to meet you all as well."

One corner of Thak's mouth twitched. He quickly grabbed his own goblet and took a long drink.

"Are you also guards?" She asked.

"Not guards in the castle but part of the army," Ograt explained.

"And are you all related?"

"Indeed we are. Siblings. Petra there's the baby of the family but truth be told she's the toughest of us all."

The young woman laughed.

"How difficult it must be for your mother."

Thak snorted and Mila immediately corrected. "I mean that you're all soldiers. Not that you're related. I only meant if something should happen in battle, it would be terrible for your mother to worry over losing all of you."

"No offense was taken, Your Highness," Ograt smiled. "Mum probably hopes a few of us would take the sword most days."

"Their mother is a commander in the army," Thak said, as if this explained everything.

"So. You're after marrying the prince, are ya?" Ograt asked in a good-natured tone. He seemed to do all the talking for the siblings.

"That is why I'm here, yes."

"And you've never met the man?"

Mila shook her head.

"Seems like a big leap of faith to offer yourself as wife to a man you know nothing about."

"I know all I need to. I know he is fierce and brave. Loyal to his people and his soldiers."

"*Aye. That's all true. But he could be cruel. He could be spiteful. He could have horrible breath. And you'd be none the wiser,*" *Ograt said.*

*Mila glanced at Thak. His lips were set in a thin hard line and his fists were clenched where they rested on the table.*

*She thought about Ograt's words, "All of those things could be true, I suppose. You're right. I'd have no way of knowing. It's why I'd hoped to meet him this evening." She looked to where the prince sat at the high table. He was currently red-faced and yelling at a serving girl. Mila's heart sank just a bit.*

"*And still you'd marry him?*" *Ograt pushed.*

"*For the people of Gildernosh, I would.*"

*Ograt nodded and called for one of the serving girls to refill his wine. The discussion was over. The next time Mila looked toward Thak, he seemed much more relaxed.*

*Over the next hour, Mila ate more than she cared to admit. The staff were constantly bringing heaping dishes to the table and Mila sampled them all. Roast pheasant with cloudberry and walnut stuffing. Gooey cheese and apricot jam. Fresh green sprouts drizzled with honey and orange zest. Small cakes and warm breads. Each dish was better than the last. When she finally felt as if she would burst, she pushed the plate aside and reached for her goblet.*

"*Glad to see you've enjoyed the kitchen's hard work,*" *Thak observed.*

"*It may have been the best meal I've ever had,*" *Mila replied honestly.*

"*Surely the wealthy kingdom of Gildernosh has decent cooks,*" *Ograt interjected.*

*Mila nodded. "We do. Just maybe not as good as the mighty kingdom of Thornscarp."*

*Ograt laughed and thumped the table. The others joined in and even Thak was close to smiling. Mila chuckled along. She was swirling the wine in her goblet when the laughter suddenly hushed. She looked up to see thunderclouds in Thak's eyes. Turning in her seat to see who deserved such a severe response, she was startled to see the prince.*

*"If you all are done playing the fools over here," he sneered, "perhaps I might borrow the princess for a dance."*

*Mila righted herself and placed her goblet on the table. "Of course, Your Highness. I would be delighted."*

*As she stood and took the prince's outstretched hand, she couldn't ignore the others. The siblings all looked as if they were preparing for battle. Their once smiling faces were now deadly calm. If Thak looked as violent as the others, she could not say. He simply stared down at his plate, refusing to meet her eyes.*

*The prince led her to the center of the hall and a small open dance space. As the musician's saw them approach, they struck up a standard waltz that was common in several kingdoms. The prince clutched one of Mila's hands in his and she placed the other on his shoulder. As he wordlessly swept her onto the floor, she caught herself studying his face.*

*Up close he was just as striking as she'd first thought. His deep brown eyes were set in a face that could have been sculpted by the heavens themselves. Full lips and high cheekbones with a strong square jaw. Golden brown hair immaculately trimmed and not a speck of dirt on his tunic. There were no horns or scales. No fur or feathers. He was perfect to look at, but dancing with him sent a different kind of unease through Mila.*

*Several other couples joined in the dance. The prince took no notice of them. Mila, however, had trouble ignoring the ugly looks sent her way. One woman, in particular, looked murderous as she twirled by. She was a petite thing, with bottle green eyes and wild raven hair. As Mila and the prince drew nearer her and her partner, Mila noted that her fingers ended in dagger-like claws. Mila made a mental note to steer clear of the woman in the future.*

*"So," the prince drawled, "you've come to snag yourself a husband, have you?"*

*Mila forced herself to smile. "An advantageous marriage would seal an alliance between our kingdoms."*

*"Advantageous? Perhaps." He looked her over and ran his tongue over his lower lip. "In some ways at least."*

*Mila swallowed against the ire rising in her. "In many ways, Your Highness. Gildernosh, as you know, has many assets that the good people of Thornscarp might benefit from."*

*He smirked. "The good people indeed."*

*"And in exchange, the military might of Thornscarp could help protect the people of Gildernosh."*

*"Hmm. Perhaps. But only if the king and queen deem you worthy."*

*Mila's brow furrowed. "Do you not have a say then?"*

*"Apparently, unlike you, in matters such as this, I do as I'm told." The music was coming to an end and Mila felt like her opportunity was slipping through her fingers.*

*"So what must I do to convince them?"*

*He barely looked at her as he released her hand. "My advice would be to act like a princess. Convince them you are actually worthy to marry their son."*

*Mila stood alone on the small dance floor as he made his way back to the high table.*

*The revelry lasted several more hours, but Mila didn't speak with the prince again. Instead, she sat quietly at the table she shared with Thak and the cat-eyed siblings. The air of joy she'd felt with them earlier had evaporated and was replaced by a quiet calm. Not unpleasant, just subdued.*

*Eventually, Mila asked if she might retire for the night. Thak nodded and rose to escort her back to her chamber.*

*"Really, it isn't necessary. I know my way. You should stay and enjoy the evening with your friends."*

*He looked at her steadily. "I insist. The queen has commanded me, and I won't neglect my duty."*

*"Of course. I'm sorry," Mila replied.*

*"Don't be."*

*They walked to her room in silence and Mila thought it odd she felt comfortable with the guard after such a short acquaintance. Despite his size and the terrifying horns and hooves, he carried himself with such grace and composure. She found herself comparing him to the handsome prince and the uncomfortable feeling she'd gotten when dancing with him. Silently, she scolded herself. It would do no good to think ill of the man she hoped to marry. It was her duty and one she would see through, if possible.*

*She had only a spare handful of days to convince the royal family she was a worthy bride but was still unsure how to accomplish the task.*

*"Thak," she said as they approached her door.*

*"Yes, Your Highness?"*

*He pushed the door open and entered her chamber, dipping his head to avoid snagging his horns.*

*Mila followed him in. "How do you suppose I might go about convincing the queen I'm a worthy bride for Prince Gregor?"*

*He turned away and knelt in front of the small hearth, arranging the blocks of peat to be lit for the fire. Mila studied the way the muscles in his back stretched beneath his tunic as he worked. She'd never seen anyone built like Thak and found herself fascinated by his movements.*

*"Should you not be trying to convince the prince himself?"*

*"Yes. I should be. But according to the prince, he has no say. It's the queen I should worry about."*

*He made a non-committal noise in response.*

*"This isn't my strong suit. Charming princes and making royals love me." She sat down on the bed, still watching Thak as he bent and stretched. He struck a match and placed it on the kindling in front. Her voice was quiet and far away when she said, "I can't even make my own father love me."*

*Thak sat back quickly, bumping his horns on the mantle above the hearth.*

*"I can't imagine that's true, Princess."*

*She smiled sadly. "You have no idea." Sitting up straighter, Mila plastered a smile on her face. "Anyway. I'm here to do what I must. So, any tips would be helpful. I feel like this is some great test and I am failing miserably."*

*"You're likely doing a much better job than you suppose." Turning full to face her, he asked. "You'd take advice from a guard?"*

*"I'd take advice from you most certainly. Why should it matter that you're a guard?"*

*He stood and walked toward the door. Just before he left, he turned his head. "It is. A test. Everything the queen does is a test. Remember that when next you speak with her. Try to get some sleep. I expect you won't sleep well."*

*The way he emphasized the words felt odd. But then again, nothing in the past day had gone as Mila had expected. She fell into bed with Thak's words, and his face, in her mind.*

# 9

*MILA* woke the following morning in a warm, comfortable bed, Thak's words from the night before still muddled in her mind. Why would he suggest she would not sleep well? The mattress was piled high with thick sumptuous layers. The comforter was warm and snug. Even the fire– which had kept her cozy the night before– had burned down and prevented the space from being stifling.

She pondered what he might have meant as she cleaned her teeth, brushed her hair and put on her now-clean traveling clothes. As expected, Thak was waiting outside her door as she emerged. Did he never sleep? She smiled, and one corner of his mouth tilted up.

"You're to meet the queen for breakfast," he said by way of greeting.

Mila stepped out into the corridor. "I'm curious as to what I ought to expect."

Once again, he was mindful of his much longer legs and adjusted his stride accordingly.

"I'd expect toast and eggs."

Was that a joke? Mila could barely contain her laugh.

Thak glanced at her and let out a long breath. "You should expect for the queen to treat you like the visiting princess you are. A guest in her home."

*"And will the prince be there?" Mila asked.*

*Thak stiffened. "I expect he won't. It's a bit on the early side for him."*

*"It isn't that early," she replied. When Thak didn't comment, she continued. "And what does he do with his days? Train with the soldiers?"*

*The big guard snorted but quickly recovered. "On a good day, he practices his swordsmanship. On many others, you're likely to find him otherwise occupied."*

*Mila thought on this as they made their way into the dining hall. Prince Gregor was known throughout all the kingdoms for his skill on the battlefield. Surely he must do some training with his men to maintain that level of ability and respect from his troops.*

*Once again, Thak pushed the door open and stepped aside so Mila could enter before him. Gone were the throngs of people and noise of the night before. No musicians greeted them. No warm candlelight danced from the walls.*

*Mila sat at a long table laden with cold meat, some cheese, and crusty bread. Several large carafes of warm tea were placed along with the food. Mila watched as Thak grabbed one and poured himself a large steaming mug of the brew. She poured herself an equally large portion and added a heavy dose of honey to it.*

*Thak chatted with another guard, then informed Mila the queen was seeing to other affairs and suggested she eat. Mila was nearly done with her breakfast when the queen was announced.*

*The princess stood and dabbed her mouth with a napkin before dipping into a curtsy as the queen sat at the head of the table.*

*"I trust you slept well?" The queen drew the statement into a question.*

Mila, unsure how to answer, flicked her eyes toward Thak. She was sure no one other than her saw the almost imperceptible movement of his head to the side.

"Uh. . . unfortunately no," Mila said. When the queen raised a single elegant eyebrow in question, she stammered. "I mean to say, I slept well enough I suppose. The room was quite comfortable, but I had difficulty calming my mind." The latter statement was true even if its implication was false. Mila still didn't understand the rules of the game she was playing.

"Interesting." The queen took a drink of her tea and studied Mila over the rim of her mug. "Dedication and duty to your people surely weigh heavily on you. Perhaps this evening you'll find better rest."

Mila assured the queen she would. The queen informed her there was to be another celebration after sundown and bid her farewell after entrusting her safety for the day to Thak once more.

She followed the enormous guard out onto the grounds of the castle in silence and was pleased when he led her toward the stables.

"Thought you might like to see the grounds on horseback."

"I'd love to, but honestly Thak, shouldn't you be resting?" The guard didn't seem tired, but surely, he must be.

"I got some sleep last night." She raised her eyebrows in surprise. "One of the other guards spelled me after you retired. I'm fine. Really."

Mila was still skeptical. "You're sure?"

"It's my duty to escort you, remember?"

"That hardly makes me feel better. But yes, I'd love to get out and have a look around."

Mila wanted to know everything there was to know about the kingdom that might one day be joined to her own. If, that was, her offer was accepted. She'd read about the *kingdom's history and had spoken with advisors in Gildernosh, but neither of those things would let her get to know the place better than experiencing it herself.*

*They spent the better part of the day exploring hidden riverbanks and small-town streets, open meadows and tiny cramped mill houses. Thak was an excellent tour guide and, while they never stopped to talk to the citizens of Thornscarp, on several occasions she saw villagers stop what they were doing to watch as they rode by. Thak talked more in that chunk of time than Mila had heard him say in the previous day. There was no way for him to hide how much he cared about the land he was raised in.*

*They returned to the castle just in time for Mila to freshen up and change for the dinner revelry.*

*The event was much as the night before, with Mila sitting and happily chatting with Thak, Ograt, and the sibling soldiers. The prince once again asked her to dance, stared at her lecherously, then bid her farewell without much conversation.*

*Just as the previous night, Thak walked her back to her chambers, said goodnight after lighting her fire, and suggested she tell the queen she was unable to sleep well, should she ask.*

*Mila, still confused, fell asleep thinking about the day and the odd behavior of both Thak and the royal family.*

*When she walked into the dining hall the following morning, the queen was waiting for her and asked how she'd slept.*

*"I feel it's impolite to say," Mila responded.*

*"Impolite?" the queen asked.*

*"Yes, Your Grace."*

*"And why would it be impolite, Princess?"*

*"Well because you all have been so welcoming to me, and the accommodations are more than adequate. But I have not been able to rest as I would at home," Mila answered.*

"I see." The queen turned to Thak. "Please make sure the princess has all that she needs to rest comfortably tonight. And do take her out again today, if you would."

Thak bowed. "Yes, my queen."

The next three days passed in much the same way. Mila spent all of her time with the guard, seeing the kingdom and chatting about her hopes and dreams. She found it oddly comforting that he would listen to her as they rode and never treated her like the pampered girl so many others did.

They were resting by a small stream when Thak informed her that they needed to head back soon in order to make it to the night's revelry.

"I don't understand why I should even attend. I'd much rather retire to my room and have a quiet dinner there, rather than get paraded around by the prince for one dance and then be cast aside like rubbish under his boots."

Thak stilled. "Is that how you truly feel?"

"Yes."

"And yet you'd still marry him?"

"I suppose I must." She plucked a small white flower from the clover where she sat and rolled it between her fingers. "It's what my people need."

"But wouldn't you rather marry for love?"

"Of course, I would Thak. But it isn't that simple. I..." She stopped talking and shook her head.

"Go on," he prompted quietly.

"I'm not sure it's appropriate to have this conversation with you, but seeing as you're my only friend here, I suppose there's little harm. You'll think I'm rather silly."

"I doubt that very much."

Thak lay back on his elbows in the clover next to her, long legs, tipped in hooves, spread out before him. His posture was relaxed, but Mila sensed the big guard could roll into motion at even the slightest threat.

*"When I came here, I had this notion that as soon as I saw the prince, I'd know my decision had been the right one. Despite all of the stories I'd heard, he would be not only handsome but also charming and full of integrity. Like you I suppose."* Mila felt Thak stiffen beside her, the conversation clearly making him uncomfortable. She sighed, then continued, *"He'd see me and know my offer of marriage was honest and pure and, maybe, he'd even find me pretty enough and companionable enough to want to marry me as well. I get* none of that *when I look at the prince."*

*"That prince is a fool,"* Thak said casually. *"You are more than pretty and your companionship is more than any man– prince or not– could hope for."*

*Mila felt a flutter in her chest at Thak's words. She turned and looked at him, but he continued to stare out over the meadow. She placed her hand over his and squeezed. "Thank you," she whispered.*

*Thak turned his head. He studied her for a moment and swallowed.*

*"We really should be getting back."*

*While they were out, someone had delivered a gown to Mila's chambers. Made of shimmering silk, the color of ocean mist, it was rather more revealing than Mila was accustomed to. Dipping low in the back and snug through her breasts, the decadent fabric set off the honey tone of her hair quite nicely. When Thak greeted her, his reaction to the gown couldn't be masked and Mila was forced to raise the back of her hand to her lips, effectively concealing her smile.*

*At the banquet, the prince once again asked her to dance. Mila agreed, but rather than trying to impress him with pretty smiles and light conversation, she went through the motions almost begrudgingly.*

"Someone's not her normal chipper self," the prince observed.

"No, I daresay, I'm not," Mila responded.

"And why might that be?"

"I suppose I'm tired. Perhaps I'll retire early this evening." The music ended and Mila turned from the handsome face of the prince before he could say another word.

Thak once again escorted her back to her chambers and lit her fire while she combed out her hair.

"Thak?" She asked as she studied the ridiculous muscles stretching across his back.

"Yes, Your Highness?"

"Why does the royal family trust you so much?"

"How do you mean, Princess?"

"Well, for starters, you've been given the task of watching over me. No chaperone, no interference from others? I'm not saying you aren't trustworthy, but does it not seem odd you're here in my chambers alone? Anything could happen."

He turned to look at her over his shoulder and Mila once again noted how handsome his face was.

"Anything?" he asked, a hint of a laugh in his voice.

"Yes." She sat up straighter on the bed. "I could make up any number of things to say and who would be the wiser?"

"You and I both know you aren't going to make up an outlandish story. Even if you did, I've known the king and queen a very long time. They'd certainly trust my word."

"I see. How long have you known them?" She pushed.

"More years than I can say."

It was an evasive answer. Thak stood and dusted off his hands. "Now, princess, you should get some rest. I'll see you in the morning."

*Mila was unhappy to see Thak go. She wanted to push him more. His answers felt true, but not entirely complete. She decided to pursue the conversation further the next day.*

*She undressed quickly and pulled on a thin silk shift. The soft cream fabric felt wonderful against her skin. She was just about to climb into bed when she heard raised voices from outside her door. She couldn't make out the words, but neither voice sounded like Thak's. Perhaps he'd already been relieved of his post and was getting some rest wherever it was he went at night.*

*She crept closer to the door just in time to hear a loud thunk and then a terrible quiet.*

*Just as she stepped forward, the door creaked open and Mila's breath caught.*

*"Hello, little princess."*

*The prince stepped over the body outside her door and into her chamber, a wicked smile stretched across his handsome face.*

♛

*The door clicked shut. Mila took several steps backward into her chamber and away from the prince. He matched her progress with his own slow predatory steps.*

*"You shouldn't be here." Mila stopped in the middle of the room. Folding her arms across her chest, she lifted her chin.*

*"Shouldn't I? I was under the impression you wanted to get to know me better."*

*"Not like this."*

*"So, you think the first time we have a private moment will be after we're wed?" He cocked one eyebrow up.*

*"No. But. . ." She didn't know what to say or how to get him out of her room. He was the prince after all. She was the one who'd thrown herself into his path.*

"But? Do you not find me handsome enough? Not princely enough? Or perhaps you wish I had horns and hooves?" The prince said the last with a sneer in his voice and on his face.

Mila's eyes widened. If she didn't know better, she'd think the prince was jealous of Thak. Jealous of a palace guard.

Well, he should be. Thak was everything the prince was not. She could just imagine the look on her father's face if she returned home with Thak. Not only part demon but a lowly guard to boot. Despite herself, the thought sent a flood of warm bubbles cascading through every inch of her, body and soul.

All traces of that warmth fled as the prince took another step toward her. Mila refused to step back again. She didn't want him to get the impression that she was running from him or, even worse, that she was moving toward the bed.

"Of course you're handsome, Your Highness. I'm sure you're quite aware of it. And I would like to get to know you better. I'm simply having trouble understanding why you think this conversation is best suited for my chambers when I'm readying myself for bed, rather than a more suitable setting like an afternoon tea."

The prince ran his tongue over his lower lip and stepped around Mila, circling her where she stood. "I'm happy you find me attractive, and I find this setting more than suitable. Aren't you curious little princess? I may have the face of an angel, but maybe my other bits are a little more demonic." He raised his brows and smirked. "Not that the other ladies have complained, but I'd hate for you to get a fright on the night of your wedding."

"With all respect for Your Highness, I'm going to have to ask that you leave." A shiver ran down Mila's spine as the prince continued his circling. He was drinking her in as he walked.

*"Oh," he crooned and drew a finger down her shoulder. "I don't think I will. We should get to know one another. After all, a man likes to know what he's signing on for."*

*The prince stopped his perusal and placed one finger below Mila's chin. She pursed her lips as he tilted her face upward. "Let's see how desperate you are to protect your people, Princess."*

*The prince wrapped one arm around her waist as his lips came down on hers. Mila tried to turn her head, but the prince used his free hand to dive into her hair and keep her facing him. His lips were brutal, and the more Mila tried to fight him, the more he seemed to enjoy the savage kiss. She opened her mouth to scream and he used it to his advantage, tugging roughly on her lower lip and chuckling as she gasped.*

Oh, she better kick his ass. Doria hurriedly turned the page.

*Mila managed to get her hands up between them and pushed against his chest, but the effort was futile. He certainly wasn't built like Thak, but he was sturdy enough. Out of other options, Mila did the only thing she could think of. With a ferocity she didn't know she possessed, she grabbed the front of the prince's tunic and used the stability of the hold to her advantage. She stepped back on one leg and then drove the other knee up as forcefully as she could, right into the prince's groin. She heard the silk of her shift rip with the thrust. The prince grunted with the impact and dropped his hands from Mila's hair and body, then doubled over trying to catch his breath.*

Thank god. Doria would have hated to throw an otherwise lovely book in the trash.

*Mila hurried to the door and threw it open. She nearly cried in relief when she saw Thak crouched on the other side, a hand on the unconscious guard's neck.*

*He looked up in surprise as she breathed his name.*

*Thak's surprise transformed into deadly calm as he looked from her face to her torn gown, and then around her to where the prince was just getting his breath back.*

*Thak's voice held barely contained rage when he spoke. "What in all the hells are you doing in the princess's room?" He straightened up and stepped around Mila. She could feel the anger pulsing off him in waves.*

*"Like you, Thak, only my duty." The prince said, anger and frustration tightening his words.*

*Thak stood with his fists clenched at his sides, looking for all the world like he'd be happy to remove the head from the prince's shoulders. The prince was not quelled by the big guard, but when Thak refused to step out of the way, Mila was surprised to see the prince avert his gaze and wait. Thak finally relented and stepped to the side, allowing the prince to exit. He didn't even glance at Mila as he walked out.*

*How had Mila ever thought him handsome? Worse, how could she willingly marry the man now? The thought of returning to Gildernosh and her father without a marriage contract to Prince Gregor in hand caused the tears which had been threatening to finally spill.*

*"Are you all right?" Thak asked quietly.*

*Mila's hand involuntarily reached to touch her lips. "It's all ruined." She swiped the tears from her cheeks. "All of it. I should have just let him…"*

*"Do not continue that thought, Your Highness."*

*Thak turned to her and pulled a lock of hair into his hand. "I'd have killed him." He twirled the stands between his fingers. "I left my flint and when I came back to retrieve it, I saw Dawson and knew something was terribly wrong."*

*The mention of the guard reminded them both of the crumpled man outside the door. They turned together to check on the unfortunate guard. He was just waking up when they reached him. Thak sat him against the wall and then jogged down the corridor. He returned with Ograt and Petra in tow. The siblings helped an apologetic Dawson to the infirmary.*

*Once they were alone again, Thak began to pace back and forth in front of the fire. Mila had grabbed one of the blankets and sat wrapped in the thick layer as she watched him.*

*Even in the close space, with Thak's energy running high, Mila marveled at how graceful he was. Despite his size and the hard texture of his hooves, he made no sound on the flagstones.*

*"Do you want to tell me what happened?" He finally asked.*

*"There isn't much to tell." Mila pulled the blanket tighter around her shoulders. "I heard them arguing and then he came in here and said we should get to know one another. He grabbed me and I acted foolishly."*

*"He put his hands on you?" Thak stopped his pacing and stared at her but didn't wait for her to answer. "You acted bravely, Mila. Not foolishly."*

*He'd never used her given name before.*

*"My bravery will cost my people dearly."*

*Thak had nothing to say to that. He came and sat next to her on the bed. "He never should have been in this room with you. Never."*

*"I was hoping to wed the man. I was so blind, ignoring all the stories, everything I'd heard about him and just hoping he would be different. I guess I would have*

*figured it all out eventually." Mila curled in on herself and rested her forehead on her knees.*

*Thak grew tense. "I need to tell you something."*

*Mila did not like the tone of his voice. She turned her head, but from her position, all she could see was a thick strong thigh. Sighing, she sat upright.*

*"Go on," she prompted.*

*"I..." he stopped and ran a palm up his forehead. "I don't really know how to explain this."*

*Mila turned more fully to face him. There was a tightening around his eyes. "I'm afraid– after everything you've gone through tonight– that when I tell you, you'll never want to speak to me again."*

*"Thak, you are the only person in this entire kingdom who has treated me with any kindness or decency. I'm sure it can't be all that bad."*

*He shook his head, pain etched on his handsome face. "Do you recall the first night we talked? I told you everything the queen does is a test?"*

*"Yes and then you prompted me to lie to her about not sleeping well, of all things. I still don't understand why that would be important. Is there a stone under the mattress or some other ridiculous thing?"*

*"You've heard about that custom then?" He smiled faintly. "No. The queen thinks you're a spoiled girl who only likes pretty things. She's convinced  you could never understand the people of Thornscarp and our demon blood. You should be disgusted by us. By this." Thak raised his hand and indicated the horns protruding from his temples.*

*Mila's hand acted on its own. She watched as it lifted and gently stroked the vicious horn from the tip down to the base where it disappeared into the loose waves of the Thak's hair. The big guard closed his eyes and a shudder ran through him. "Mila," he groaned.*

*"Sorry," she whispered. "I shouldn't have done that."*

*Thak took her hand and it disappeared in his much larger one. "If you do that again, I'm not responsible for what might happen next."*

*"Why does that make me very much want to do it again?" Mila smiled. "When I first came here, I didn't know what to expect. And yes, it was a bit unnerving when we first met. Not just you. The guard with the feathers? She is terrifying."*

*Thak chuckled.*

*"But then I got over my initial shock and I got to spend time with you. If the prince were half the man you are, I wouldn't care if he had a tail and a forked tongue. He's beautiful to look at, but under the surface, he's vile." Thak grunted in agreement.  "I still don't know why I'm lying to the queen though."*

*"She dangled that handsome bastard in front of you. In her eyes, all you care about is the shiny handsome prince. You should be able to rest easy, even if you know nothing about him. If you're worried about marrying someone who is easy on the eyes, but treats you poorly, maybe there's more to you than meets the eye."*

*Mila suddenly understood. The queen wanted her to fail, and what better way to fail than to agree to a marriage based solely on her desperation and what she saw on the surface?*

*"But what does that have to do with you?"*

*"I'm part of the test, Mila."*

*"She wanted to see if I could put your appearance aside and still spend time with you?" she guessed.*

*"Yes, but it's a little deeper than that."*

*"Tell me."*

*"When you asked the prince before if he had a say in the decision about the marriage, he told you the truth. He does not."*

*Mila nodded.*

*"He doesn't have a say. But I do."*

*Mila's brow furrowed. Why would a guard have a say in who the prince was to marry?*

*Thak looked away from the question in her eyes. "The royal family trusts me with you Mila, because I am part of the royal family. Thak is short for Thakary. It's a family name. My full title is Prince Gregor Thakary Thorn, otherwise, I'm known as Prince Gregor the Mightly of Thronscarp"*

*There was a swirling storm in Mila's head, and she was having trouble focusing. Memories rushed back to her from the previous days. Thak escorting her through the kingdom. Thak's love for the villages and the people. The easy way the guards and soldiers interacted with him. The queen's trust in Thak watching over Mila during her time among them. All of them mixed and shifted and blurred in her mind.*

*Thak was Prince Gregor. Thak was who she'd offered herself to in marriage. Thak was the one destined to be King of Thornscarp and who could help her protect her own people.*

*"Your Highness. Mila. Say something. Please." His tone was anxious.*

*"I... I don't know what exactly to say," she finally responded. Mila stood and began to walk a looping path around the room. "I don't understand. You've been lying to me. All this time. You let me believe you were just a guard and that the prince was. . . Wait a minute. If you're the prince, who is...?" She trailed off, remembering what could have happened if things had gone differently earlier. Her stomach turned.*

*"That bastard—Stefan—is a prince. Just not the prince. He's my brother. And I think I might hurt him very badly after what he pulled."*

*"Your brother?" Mila was growing more agitated. She knew the name Stefan. He had a very different reputation than Gregor. The feckless younger brother to the mighty soldier was known through the kingdoms as a young man who loved the drink and the ladies a bit too much. "All this time you were playing with me. And what if I'd given in to him just now? Would you have laughed in my face then thrown me out? Was that the test?"*

*"No. Mila. I swear I didn't think he'd ever try something like that. If my mother knew what he'd done, she'd be just as furious as I am."*

*"But this is all some big game to you and your family." Mila ran to her pack and snatched it up from where it rested on the floor. Throwing open the wardrobe she began grabbing her things and shoving them in. She needed to be gone from this castle and away from the people and demons who called it home.*

*"Mila, please. I know you're angry. But listen to me." Thak– or Gregor– came to stand near her. "This wasn't my idea. And while my mother may have gone about things wrong, she did it for the right reasons."*

*Mila shot upright. "The right reasons? You can't be serious. What reason could possibly justify my humiliation like this?"*

*"She is protective of her kingdom. And of me."*

*"As if you need protecting! Everyone knows the stories of Prince Gregor. The prince, beloved by his soldiers and bane to those who oppose him on the battlefield."*

*"I am a force at war, it's true. But you have no idea how many lovely young women have walked through those doors claiming to be of royal blood. How many fathers have paraded their daughters in front of my parents, only to turn green when they see me and realize it's a monster they thought to unite with their precious daughters."*

Mila's rage lost some of its edge as he spoke. "It's because they don't know you. The real you," she said.

"And would you have taken the time to get to know the real me before you fled from my sight that first night?"

"Of course," she responded immediately then paused. "Or at least, I think I would have."

She thought back to her arrival at the castle and how her tears had flowed once she was alone in her chambers. The guard with the feathers, the soldiers with scales, and– Thak. Thak with his horns and hooves. It was only after being around his quiet confidence and gentle grace that she'd gotten past those things. Maybe the queen had been right. Maybe she didn't deserve him at all.

The prince– the real prince– must have seen the conflict on her face. He stepped forward and placed a gentle hand below her chin. He tilted her face upward and looked into her eyes. Mila felt that look all the way in her toes. "I understand if you can never forgive me. But I certainly hope that you might."

"Can you forgive me?" Mila asked.

"And what do I need to forgive you for?"

"For coming here, to your home, begging you to marry me, and not being the kind of person I thought I was."

"Hmm. Not many of us are always the person we strive to be. But we keep striving nonetheless." He ran his hand from her chin up the side of her face and into her hair. "If it helps to sway you, Ograt considers you divine."

Mila chuckled and melted into his touch. She raised her hand and once again let her fingers trail from the tip of his horn down to the base. He groaned in response.

"What should I call you?" She asked. "Your Highness, as you insist with me? Thak? Gregor?"

"My subjects call me Your Highness– so definitely not that. Gregor is my formal name, but my family and close friends call me Thak. If you wish to do the same, I won't *object. But," he paused and closed his eyes as she stroked her hand down his horn again, "I'd really rather you call me your husband."*

*Mila started in surprise. "Are you agreeing to my offer then?"*

*"How can I refuse? You're courageous and kind. You're dedicated to your people and I'm sure you'll be the same with mine. Add in your beauty, the way you look in that thin silk gown, and what you're doing to me right now," he sighed as she stroked her hands down through his hair and over his shoulders, "and you certainly pass the test."*

*He grinned when her hands stilled. "But could you love me?"*

*"I already do, Mila."*

*"That's unfortunate," she responded seriously. Thak frowned. "I can't marry a prince when I've already fallen in love with a royal guard."*

*She sent him a teasing smile.*

*Mila yelped when Thak wrapped his strong arms around her and lifted her off her feet. He carried her to the bed and cradled her as he climbed onto the mattress and lay down with her on top of him. Mila didn't wait before she stretched along his solid body and kissed him. He tasted like warm spiced wine and Mila could envision herself getting just as drunk on him.*

*Thak shifted below her, and she pushed up onto her elbows.*

*"You know, I think my mother has done something to this bed," Thak grumbled and reached under the mattress to retrieve a large heart-shaped stone. He raised it up and showed it to Mila.*

*"What on earth is that?" She asked. "And why didn't I feel it?"*

*Thak grinned as he shook his head. "I thought you'd heard the old grannies' tales. It's an old superstition in*

Thornscarp. If you place a hearthstone in someone's bed, their true nature will be revealed. As for why you didn't feel it?" He shrugged. "You must be a deep sleeper. I really hope you don't snore."

Mila smiled down at him. His expression turned from light and teasing to hungry and intense in a blink. She wondered at how he'd been keeping himself in check the past few days and decided she wanted to see that expression every day for the rest of her life.

The fabric of her shift pulled tight against her body and she needed to free herself from it. Rising up, she straddled him and pulled the gown off over her head. Mila was rewarded with the sharp intake of Thak's breath. He lay still beneath her and stared up at her uncovered body.

"You are glorious, Mila. So much so, it almost hurts to look at you." His voice was deep and husky. Mila felt the blush warming her cheeks. "Just stay there a moment. I want to capture this in my memory."

When she could take it no longer, she bent forward and began kissing him again. Thak ran his hands up her legs and cupped her backside, causing her to moan into his mouth. It seemed to undo his restraint. In one fluid motion, he rolled her beneath him then stood and removed his own clothing. Now it was Mila's turn to gasp in surprise. He was superb. Each muscle defined as if he'd been sculpted from marble. She drank in his perfection. She loved his demon attributes just as much as his human ones and the part she was focused on in that moment was certainly human. Although it's size matched the rest of him.

When she'd had her fill, she grabbed his hands and pulled him back into the bed with her, already smiling at the thought of not having to lie to the queen about her lack of sleep.

The following morning, when Mila and Thak met with the queen over breakfast, the prince announced his plans to *marry Mila as soon as the arrangements could be made. There was a shift in the royal family at the news. While not openly warm and welcoming, Mila got a definite sense of well-earned acceptance from them. Stefan had the good sense to stay away from his brother in the following days and Thak was more than happy to accompany Mila on her journey home to break the news to her father. Ograt and his siblings were downright giddy when they heard the news and the bald, pierced soldier agreed to her request to have him and his siblings promoted to her personal guard.*

*Mila couldn't stop smiling at her good fortune. She had done just what she'd set out to do and managed to find her very own demon prince in the process.*

# 10

WELL then. Not quite the demon monsters Doria had planned on, but she actually really liked it. And she wasn't just saying that, seeing as she was the one to pick the book. There were bits she might have changed, like making it longer for example. She could actually see it getting fleshed out into a full-length novel. That might be worth a read.

She made a mental note of the author's name—it wasn't someone she'd read before—and packed the book up in her satchel.

The sun was just settling over the buildings to the west and the first flicker of a bright star could be seen in the east. It was the perfect time to visit Vespertine Books.

As she made her way out of the park, she felt eyes on her. Turning to look over her shoulder, she scanned the few faces lingering on the grass or at the playground. None seemed to be turned in her direction. Going a few steps further, she felt it again. She was shaking her head and chiding herself for a fool when a dark shadow stepped from the trees to her right. She startled and raised her hands before she realized that she recognized the man. Peter Smith—the only soul other than Cassie and Miles that she'd ever seen inside of the bookshop.

"Ah. Ms. James," he said. "How fortunate to see you this evening."

Doria blinked, momentarily disoriented by his sudden arrival. "Hello, Peter. Funny meeting you here." She tried for a joking tone, but even in her own ears, it sounded weak.

"Call it coincidence. Or fate, perhaps," he replied, leaning into her space. "But I've been thinking about you quite a lot recently. How's the reading going?"

"Quite well actually. In fact, I just finished a five-star read and was heading to Vespertine to discuss it with Miles," Doria explained. There was a strange tension emanating from Peter but she couldn't say why exactly.

"Interesting. And what book would that be?"

"Oh, I've got it right here." She reached into her bag and fished out the first thing she touched. When she pulled it up, however, she realized it was the book she'd borrowed from the library.

Peter glanced down at it and a shadow skimmed across his face. Frowning, he looked up at her. "Now, what would you be doing reading something like this?"

Doria looked down, confused by his change in tone. "Oh, it's just something I grabbed for my roommate. She loves the town and is always looking to learn more about it." She shoved the library book back in her bag, not sure exactly why she lied, but feeling it was the right thing to do. "This is the book I meant. You should give it a try sometime."

The frown still hadn't left Peter's face. "That's not really my cup of tea I'm afraid. I don't read trash."

"It's hardly trash Peter. But. . ." she shrugged.

Doria's instincts were telling her to get away from this man as quickly as she could. "Well, I should be getting on. Miles is expecting me."

Peter's lips tilted up, but the smile didn't reach his eyes. "Oh, I don't think so. Not tonight, he isn't." Without any further explanation, Peter Smith turned and walked into the deepening shadows of the park.

Doria didn't wait to see where he was going. She hurried to the crosswalk and darted across the street. Making her way past the bar and to the alcove where the bookshop should have been, she found a blank brick wall once more.

"You have got to be shitting me," she mumbled. She paced up and down the block several more times, hoping as the night drew darker the sign would somehow appear. After several more passes, it seemed Peter was right. Miles was not waiting for her. Putting her head down, she headed home.

Doria woke in a foul temper. She had really hoped to see Miles the night before. The run-in with Peter Smith mixed with the lingering effects of the dream she'd had about Miles and the fact Cassie seemed to be withholding some sort of information about the situation, combined to make for one hell of a mood.

Knowing it was probably futile, she walked the distance to where the bookshop should have been. Its repeated absence did nothing to brighten her spirits. Heading back to the library, she plopped down at a reading table and dove into the book she'd checked out the day before. It was full of interesting bits and pieces of local lore and everything from interesting tales of witch trials, supposedly haunted hotels, and even a ghost dog that was known to frequent the cemetery on the hill heading out of town.

Doria rubbed between her eyes and pushed back in her chair. None of this was helping her get any closer to the mystery that was Miles and his shop.

Determined not to give up just yet, she flipped to the index and scanned the listing for the name "Vespertine Books". Nothing was there and Doria's frustration grew. She ran her fingers down the text and startled when she saw 'Oak, Miles' in tiny print. The book didn't have any recent history included, but it didn't mean Miles didn't have parents or grandparents who were an intricate part of the town's history.

Quickly, she flipped to the page listed and was surprised to see an old black-and-white image of a smiling man standing in front of a small shop front. The resemblance to her Miles was uncanny. The family genes must run strong and when had he become *her Miles*? It was hard to judge the date of the photo-based solely on the man. He wore tailored trousers and a button-up shirt, but that could mean any time frame from the thirties to the sixties. If he'd been a woman, it might have been easier for Doria to peg.

She looked down and read the caption below.

*Local businessman, Miles Oak, pictured above at the opening of his doomed bookstore, has been said to haunt the streets of the town since his disappearance and presumed death in the catastrophic fire which destroyed his beloved business. Several residents have claimed to see the specter over the decades, most claiming he is seeking revenge on the man who took his life.*

*Local legend states, shortly after purchasing the shop, Oak got into a heated disagreement with a fellow businessman and, in a fit of rage, the other man set the bookshop ablaze, trapping Oak inside. The store was completely consumed before rescuers could arrive and no remains of the well-liked store owner were ever found.*

*So, if you wander the streets late at night and see the handsome Miles Oak roaming, best to leave him be. You never know if the ghastly specter will mistake you for the man who destroyed him and take his wrath out on an unsuspecting innocent victim.*

Doria blinked at the book a few times. Miles must be related to the man in the photo.

A chill ran down her spine. Her brain was trying to tie things together and the conclusion it wanted to jump to was absurd. Was this man *actually* Miles? And if they were the same person, did that mean he was a ghost? She shut the thought down as soon as it surfaced. She wasn't a fucking idiot and this wasn't some sexy paranormal romance. This was real life. *Her* real life. And there had to be a legitimate and reasonable explanation.

Obviously, there was more to the tale and Doria was determined to get to the bottom of it.

Placing a scrap of paper in the book to mark the page, Doria closed the cover and slipped it into her bag. Then she pulled out her phone and did a quick internet search for Miles and the town legend. Nothing new came up. Trying another tactic, she searched for a current business listing. Nothing there either. Not a website or even a phone number for the bookstore. No Yelp reviews, not a single social media post about the amazing space. Surely someone would have tagged the place if they'd been there. It seemed Felicity wasn't the only one who had never heard of the spot. With mounting frustration, she locked the screen and gathered her belongings.

She still had her meeting with Cassie and Elenor that evening. One way or another, she'd figure this thing out.

Doria and Felicity stepped onto the garden path leading to the old cottage, its brick walls turning a rosy hue in the last rays of sunlight. The vibrant greens and blues of flowers glistened in the twilight, and the scent of early spring blooms lingered in the air. Doria brushed past a low-hanging branch as they rounded the corner, revealing the two-story cottage that might help her unravel another tiny sliver of the mystery.

On the way over, Doria had explained what she'd found in the borrowed library book. Felicity had remained quiet as she relayed the legend.

"I think I remember that one from when I was a kid. Particularly around Halloween, the nerds I hung out with would say they saw the ghost wandering the streets at night. It was all bullshit of course, but I wonder." Felicity smiled wickedly at her friend.

"You wonder what?" Doria asked.

"I wonder how hot ghost sex could be! You'll have to let me know." She bumped shoulders with Doria and kept walking.

"Remind me again why I invited you along."

"Because you love me, Peaches!"

Doria laughed as they walked, but the closer to the edge of town they got, the more worried she became. She'd felt like she was starting to make a real connection with Miles and the cozy shop. At least when she could find it. She still feared this was all in her head and she might be slowly going crazy. They'd reached the address Cassondra had sent and now stood at the gate leading through the garden to the house.

Felicity must have sensed her friend's mood. "Are you sure about this?" she asked, her green eyes reflecting her concern as they walked up the path toward the front door.

Doria took a deep breath, her dark eyes scanning the area. "We need answers, Felicity," she replied, her voice firm despite the uncertainty clawing at her chest.

Cassondra opened the door and warm light spilled out, accompanied by a chorus of creaking floorboards. She smiled in relief when she saw them. "Oh, you made it." She motioned for them with her hands. "Come on in!"

They followed her into the quaint living room, where candles flickered, casting dancing shadows upon the walls. An elderly woman sat in an armchair by a cold fireplace, knitting needles clicking away rhythmically and a puff of white hair encircling her head. She peered over her wire-rimmed glasses from where she was perched on her chair, metal and yarn in hand. Her bright eyes lit up as the two young women stepped through the threshold of her home.

"Ah, you must be Doria and Felicity," she said, her voice strong and clear despite her age. "I'm Elenor."

"Nice to meet you, Elenor," Felicity said, her natural warmth shining through as she extended a hand.

"Likewise," Doria added cautiously, studying the old woman's features. She couldn't shake the feeling that there was more to Elenor than met the eye. But, then again, wasn't that why they were there?

"Please, sit down," Elenor gestured to the empty chairs opposite her. As they settled in, she continued knitting, her eyes never leaving them. "Cassondra has told me a great deal about you Doria."

Doria wasn't sure how to respond. "Only good things, I hope," she said with a chuckle, trying to ease the tension that hung thick in the air.

"Of course," Cassondra replied, offering a reassuring smile. "The moment you walked into Vespertine Books, I knew there was something special about you."

Doria's clenched her hands into fists at her sides, her impatience growing. "Speaking of which, I'm desperate to know anything you can tell me about Miles," she blurted out, unable to contain herself any longer.

Elenor's gaze sharpened, her knitting needles pausing mid-stitch. She glanced at Cassondra, who nodded solemnly in response. The old woman turned her attention back to Doria, a wide smile blossoming across her face.

"Would you ladies like some tea?" Elenor asked, her voice tinged with an edge of mischief.

"Uh, sure," Felicity replied hesitantly, exchanging glances with Doria.

"Or perhaps something stronger?" Elenor suggested, arching a slender, silver eyebrow, a twinkle in her eye. There was something about the look that reminded Doria so much of Miles when he was teasing her about books. "Maybe a little something to warm us up a bit first. Something tells me we're going to need it," she said, a wicked grin spreading across her wrinkled face. "Especially if we're discussing Miles and his...peculiar bookstore."

Before they could answer, the feisty old lady rolled out a drinks cart from behind her armchair, its polished surface gleaming in the fading light. Bottles clinked together as she began mixing gin and tonics with surprising vigor.

"I'll have mine neat, please," Doria said without missing a beat.

Elenor nodded approvingly and, soon enough, four glasses were filled to the brim - one for each of them. "To getting down to business," she said as they all clinked their glasses together and took a sip.

The fiery liquid burned all the way down but instantly warmed Doria's chest.

The elderly woman cleared her throat before beginning, "It may come as a bit of a shock to you, but Miles and I are, in fact, related."

Doria recalled Miles referring to Elenor as being *like* a sister to him. Grandmother seemed more accurate though and he certainly hadn't said he *was* related to her.

"A great nephew or something?" She asked for clarity's sake.

Elenor paused to take another sip of her drink before continuing, "Not exactly. I'm his niece."

Doria choked on her drink.

Oh god. The book was right. He was a ghost.

Cassondra shifted uncomfortably in her seat, reluctance evident in her furrowed brow. "I'm not sure that was the best way to break the ice, Elenor."

"He's a ghost, isn't he?" Doria asked.

"A ghost!" Elenor gasped between fits of laughter. "Oh, that's rich!"

Even Cassie chuckled, wiping tears from her eyes. Felicity grinned sheepishly, while Doria struggled to hide her embarrassment. She hadn't expected this reaction. What had she missed?

"Forgive us, dear," Elenor said, finally regaining her composure. "It's just not what we were expecting you to say."

"Then what is he?" Doria demanded, her face burning with a mix of humiliation and curiosity. "You gave me that book, and when I saw the description in it, I just thought. . .Then you tell me you're," she looked pointedly at Elenor, "his niece. How else could that family tree work?"

Cassondra's laughter died down, and she exchanged a serious glance with Elenor. The old woman took a deep breath, the weight of untold secrets pressing down on her shoulders.

"Let me assure you, Miles is no ghost," she began, her voice firm despite the lingering traces of amusement in her eyes. "But his situation is...complicated."

Doria felt her heart pounding against her rib cage as if it was trying to escape. She could hardly believe she had mustered the courage to ask these women, who sat before her like sphinxes, for answers about Miles and the strange bookstore that had captivated her imagination. A chill spread over her skin as she waited breathlessly for their response.

"Tell me everything," she said, her eyes locked onto Elenor's, teeth gritted and fingers digging into the armrests of her chair.

Elenor took a slow sip of her gin and tonic, the ice clinking against the glass as if it were a secret code. The setting sun cast long shadows across the room, giving it an otherworldly feel. Doria felt her heart race in anticipation of the story she was about to hear.

"Alright," Elenor began, setting her drink down on the table with a decisive clink. "Miles is alive, but he's been bound by magic to that bookstore for seventy-five years."

"Seventy-five years?" Felicity gasped, her green eyes wide with shock. "How is that even possible?"

"Magic can be cruel, dear," Elenor replied, a hint of sadness in her voice. "He's trapped inside, able to leave only once a year."

"Wait," Doria interjected, her brows furrowing in confusion. "Only once a year. Otherwise, he's just in there? Like a genie in a bottle?"

Doria was surprised at how easy it was to accept this ridiculous story. Down deep she knew there was something otherworldly at play, and this explanation made as much sense as anything else, but seventy-five years? He was old enough to be her. . . she refused to allow that train of thought. Not when he looked like a man in the prime of his life.

"Once a year," Cassondra agreed. "And only on the anniversary of the night he was bound."

Those must have been the nights when the locals claimed to have seen him. No wonder he got the ghostly reputation.

"He doesn't age and he doesn't die. He's just there."

"It must be torture for him." Doria barely whispered the words.

"We try to visit as often as we can. Bring him news and company. Occasionally someone will wander in if the shop sees fit to allow it. But for us, it's getting harder and harder," Elenor said. "It's been months since I was there."

"Why?" Felicity asked. "Can't you pop in and out whenever you like?"

"Ah," Cassondra chimed in, her expression grim. "The entrance to the store doesn't always appear in the same place, and it's become increasingly difficult to find over the years. Elenor has difficulty walking around looking for it. And it only seems to present itself to those with a special connection to Miles."

"But I found it the first time easily. And since then, it's always been in the same spot, if it's there at all."

Felicity, ever the curious one, posed the question that had been burning at the edges of Doria's mind. "How do you know all this? And if Elenor is Miles' niece, what's your connection to him, Cassie?"

Elenor's gaze softened, and she looked at both Felicity and Doria with a mixture of sorrow and determination. "I know this because I am Miles' niece. I was only ten years old when he was trapped." She paused, taking a deep breath before continuing. "Cassondra here is his granddaughter."

Doria's stormy eyes filled with tears, threatening to spill over as she absorbed the gravity of Miles' situation. She'd grown fond of him in their short time together, and the thought of him trapped by a curse for so long was unbearable. And yet, another pang of jealousy shot through her chest at the mention of him having a granddaughter. If he had a granddaughter, then he had a child and that meant he'd been someone's husband. How could she ever compete with a ghost from his past?

"Are you saying that...Miles was married?" Doria asked hesitantly, her voice cracking under the weight of her emotions. She couldn't look at Cassondra or Elenor, afraid they might see her vulnerability.

"He was for a brief time. It wasn't a happy marriage. You must remember this was years ago and things were different then. One bad decision led to a rushed wedding, and shortly after the child was born, his mother ran off with some piece of human waste. Miles was left to raise the child on his own." Elenor explained, her voice gentle but firm. "It was a great tragedy and it left him heartbroken for his son but not for himself. Cassondra's father came to live with us when Miles was bound to the shop. He became my brother essentially. He was three years old."

"My father visited him almost every day as he grew up. It was a kind of torture for them both. Dad passed away last year," Cassondra said with a sigh. "Now it's just Elenor and myself who know about Miles. And now you."

Doria's thoughts swirled like a tempest, struggling to process this revelation. How had she become entangled in such a complex web of magic and family secrets? The weight of the situation pressed down on her, but she knew she couldn't turn away from it now.

"Is there any way to break this curse?" Doria asked, her voice barely more than a whisper. She looked at Elenor, hoping for some hint of a solution, some sliver of hope that Miles could be freed from his magical prison.

"Over the years, we've tried everything we could think of," Cassondra replied, her voice heavy with the burden of her family's past. "But nothing has worked...yet."

"Yet?" Felicity echoed, her eyes shining with curiosity and hope.

Elenor glanced at Doria, her gaze piercing like a spear through the shadows of the room. "We believe that you, dear, may hold the key to freeing Miles. You are the only one who seems to find the store so easily, as if drawn to it by some unseen force."

The words hung in the air, a challenge and an invitation all at once. Doria felt the pull of destiny tugging at her heart, urging her to step forward and embrace her role in this magical tale.

Miles was trapped. He'd seen his only child grow old and die. He was kept from the outside world and all its changes, except for one night a year, and through the second-hand news he received, from the books in his shop, and the people he loved. And yet, he'd always seemed so full of life and positivity. Quick to smile and to tease.

"Alright," she whispered, her gaze meeting Elenor's with newfound resolve. "I'll help you free Miles. Whatever it takes."

As the sun dipped below the horizon, casting long shadows across the room, Doria knew that her life was about to change in ways she could never have anticipated.

# 11

AFTER leaving the little cottage on the edge of town, Doria's head was spinning. She wanted to walk awhile to clear it. Curses and bindings. Magic and relative immortality. It was all a little too much to take in. Knowing her friend would need some space, Felicity parted ways with her near the park and told her she'd be waiting at home when Doria was ready to talk.

It came as no surprise when Doria's feet took her on a path to where she'd entered the bookshop before. After all the night's revelations, she was more than a little surprised when the worn wooden sign made itself known and the doorknob turned easily in her hand.

She hadn't seen him since the night she'd dreamed about them together.

The light inside was dimmer than it had been before, and the flickering of candles caused shadows to dance upon the walls. It made sense Miles wouldn't care about the flames. It was a bubble of magic which kept the shop intact. Presumably, nothing as mundane as fire would destroy it.

Doria had so many questions. How did the new books arrive? Did Miles have control over any of it? Where did he get his groceries? Was there a hidden apartment somewhere where he could rest, bathe, and keep up that impeccable appearance when he needed to? Had he really read every single book in the place?

All of her questions flew from her mind when she saw him. Miles glanced up from a stack of books he was shelving. For a moment, they just stared at each other, a tense silence filling the space between them. Then Miles set down the books and walked over to her.

"I'm glad you came back," he said softly.

Doria swallowed hard, trying to ignore the warmth flooding her at his words. "I tried to yesterday, but..." she held up her hands in a poof gesture. "We have unfinished business to discuss."

A slow smile spread over his chiseled face and Doria's mind flashed back to the dream she'd had of him.

She needed to talk to him about so many things, but in the moment, all she wanted to do was look at him. His dark hair and light eyes. The way his cheek dimpled when he smiled. The quiet confidence he had when he challenged her on everything from books to life. All of it drew her toward him where he waited inside the shop.

But Doria was who she was, and she would never forgive herself if she just gave in to the physical being that he was. Some things were more important than lust and attraction.

Stepping closer, she stopped before him, her chest tight. She searched his face, noticing new lines of worry creasing his brow, and swallowed. "We need to talk."

"Ok." His frown deepened.

"You're hiding something from me," she said quietly.

Miles sighed and ran a hand through his hair, tousling the dark strands. "I am. But not because I  want to. I can't tell you everything." He ran a hand through his hair and took a deep breath. "That isn't right. I *don't want* to tell you everything. My life is just. . . Well, it isn't normal, and I cannot bear the thought of scaring you off."

His words resonated with truth, as did the emotion in his eyes. Doria wanted so badly to believe him.

She nodded.

On second thought, she wasn't sure she could do this right now. Maybe she needed more time to process. He had been married and had a child. He was decades old. Not to mention there was some unspoken curse on him. Panic rising, she cursed herself for the coward she was and said lightly, "You knew that book wasn't a horror novel."

He barked a laugh and the tension broke just a little.

"Is that really what you want to talk about?"

"Yes. No." She looked down at her hands. Miles's gentle fingers found her chin and tilted her eyes up to meet his own.

"I think the book can wait. I was pretty thrilled when you chose it though. I'll sway you to the dark side eventually. Or the light side, as the case may be." He smirked and she smiled back. Despite everything she learned, there was still something about him that made her feel lighter. Happier. Less angry at the world and her place in it..

He studied her a moment. "I'd give just about anything to know what you're thinking right now."

Unbidden, the image of him shirtless filled her mind. She *was not* going to tell him about her dream. Under any circumstances. As if reading her mind, he raised a brow and said, "I had the most amazing dream the other night. Would you care to hear about it?"

Doria's heart fluttered. He couldn't know. And he couldn't have dreamt the same thing.

"I was here. And you were here. And we were discussing literature." The way he said it made it sound naughty and filthy and perfect in all the right ways. "And there was this tension in the air. Kind of like now. " He stepped forward and ran a finger along her collarbone.

Doria grabbed his wrist and pushed the sleeve of his shirt up to reveal the barest traces of dark black ink. She drew in a deep breath and let it out slowly.

"It... how? No." She shook her head. "No?" He whispered into her hair. "You don't like it? To be fair, neither do I."

Doria loved tattoos and she'd certainly loved the look of his in her dream. She shook her head. "In my dream, I thought it was pretty fucking sexy actually."

He smiled. "I'm glad someone thinks so. But it wasn't just your dream. It was our dream. I had the same one."

Had they really shared the same dream? It didn't seem possible, but everything she'd experienced in the last few days had been impossible. Why should this be any different?

Doria stepped back and tilted her chin to his chest. "Take it off."

He chuckled but complied. He undid each button in slow deliberate movements, never taking his eyes from her face. Doria licked her lower lip, heat pooling in her core.

He slipped the fabric down over his shoulders and Doria stepped forward to trace the lines of script making up the tattoo covering him from wrist to collarbone. "I saw this. In my dream." She couldn't help but repeat herself.

He nodded.

"How did I see this in my dream?"

"It's all rather complicated."

"People keep saying that," Doria grumbled.

"People?"

"I met with Elenor and Cassie. They explained a few things."

Miles stilled and his face grew tight.

Doria's voice was breathy as she said, "We have a lot to talk about."

Again, he nodded.

"The funny thing is, I don't want to talk right now," Doria murmured.

He let out a long breath.

Before she could react, Miles closed the distance between them in two swift strides. He grasped her face in his hands and brought his lips down on hers.

Doria gasped, a jolt of heat and desire igniting within her at his touch. She should push him away, should demand answers, but his fingers slid into her hair, and she was lost. Her eyes drifted shut as she kissed him back, timidly at first, then with growing hunger.

Miles groaned. "Do you want this?" he whispered against her lips. "Do you want me?"

"Yes," she breathed, though she knew she shouldn't. There were too many secrets still between them, too much left unsaid. But in that moment, she didn't care. She wanted Miles more than she wanted her next breath.

Something tugged at her mind. He'd had a child. Elenor had said it wasn't planned, but his love for his son had been torture for him. "Give me just a sec." She ran to her bag and pulled out the strip of foil packets Felicity had gifted her. "I've got these."

"Good." Miles traced a line of kisses down her throat, his hands roaming over her body and leaving trails of fire in their wake. "Because I haven't stopped thinking about you since I first set eyes on you."

Doria shuddered, desire and apprehension warring within her. She didn't know Miles, not really, and yet she was powerless to resist him. All she knew was that she needed him, and if it meant confronting difficult truths later, then so be it.

Right now, all that mattered was losing herself in his embrace.

Miles kissed her slowly, then began the slow torture of peeling away her clothes, layer by layer, until Doria stood bare before him. She flushed under his heated gaze, unable to stop herself from crossing her arms over her chest. His eyes softened and he stepped forward, wrapping his hands around hers and tugging them away from her body.

"Don't hide from me," he murmured, pressing a gentle kiss to each of her knuckles. "Please don't hide. You're beautiful."

Doria felt something inside her melt at his words and she dropped her arms to her sides, allowing Miles to drink in the sight of her. His eyes darkened, the pupils dilating as they roamed over her. He ran his fingertips lightly over the curves of her waist and hips, then back up to cup her neck as he captured her lips once again. Every nerve in Doria's body was alive and buzzing. She shivered with the pure pleasure of being touched.

Miles's hands drifted lower, circling first Doria's breast before trailing down her stomach to her hips once more. His fingers slid over the sensitive skin of her thighs, tracing a path up and down with each pass until she was trembling with anticipation. His lips followed in the wake of his hand and soon his tongue and teeth were bringing her the most exquisite pleasure she had ever experienced.

Doria felt as though she was on a different plane of existence; every touch from Miles brought her closer to the edge of something unknown. Her breathing grew ragged as Miles explored her body, intensifying when he finally settled his hand between her legs and began to work his magic. She gasped at the sensation of him exploring every inch of her, pushing past any remaining barriers and leaving only pleasure in its wake.

Soon Doria was spinning out of control, waves of pleasure crashing over her as Miles continued to drive forward.

Just when she thought she couldn't take anymore, Miles shifted his hand and drug his thumb along the perfect spot. The intensity built until, finally, Doria shattered around him, crying out in bliss as wave after wave of pleasure flooded through her body.

Miles held her up as her legs went loose beneath her. When she finally caught her breath, she laughed, "I guess you have been reading the right books after all."

"You have no idea. I'm just getting started," he teased back.

Emboldened, Doria reached for the fastenings of his pants. Miles sucked in a sharp breath as she
deftly undid the buttons of his trousers and eagerly parted the zipper, revealing a taut length. She slowly curled her hand around him, feeling his heat as he gasped in pleasure.

Miles tilted her chin up and captured her mouth in a searing kiss, banishing all doubts from her mind. Doria stroked him firmly, swallowing his groans of pleasure.

"Doria James," he growled, breaking the kiss. His eyes flashed with mingled desire and warning. "It's been awhile for me. Keep doing that, and this will be over before it's begun."

Doria smirked, a thrill running through her at his loss of control. "Then we'll just have to take our time," she purred, dragging her nails up the length of him in a slow delicious stroke.

Miles' eyes narrowed. In one swift movement, he pinned her against the wall, hands on either side of her head. "Time is one thing I've got plenty of," he said hoarsely. "Time to hear you moaning again. Time to savor each and every inch of you."

Doria's heart pounded as Miles lifted her onto the edge of a bookshelf, his strong arms supporting her weight. She wrapped her legs around his waist, gasping as he came in full contact with her body.

"The books," she breathed.

"Will survive," he answered. "Though I might not, if I wait much longer."

Miles' muscles quivered beneath her fingertips as he moved them both closer to the edge of the shelf. He kissed her deeply, their tongues tangling.

Doria tilted her head back and her eyes drifted closed.

"Look at me," Miles commanded softly. Doria met his gaze, startled by the intensity in his pale eyes. "I want to see your face when I'm inside you."

Without warning, he thrust into her, sheathing himself to the hilt. Doria cried out at the sudden intrusion, nails digging into his shoulders. Miles held himself still, watching her face closely.

"God but you're perfect," he groaned. "So perfect."

Miles moved slowly at first, allowing Doria to savor every inch of him before gradually increasing his pace until they were both panting with desire. His hands caressed her body and then trailed down to firmly grip one of hers, interlocking their fingers as they moved together as one perfect entity.

Her whole world narrowed to the feel of him moving inside her, the scrape of the shelf against her back, and Miles' heated gaze. His name spilled from her lips over and over.

Miles moved faster, harder. "That's it," he panted, "let go for me, Doria."

Doria could feel herself building up to climax and she desperately tried to hold on for just a few moments more; wanting to keep this moment alive forever.

But it was too late, and with one final thrust from Miles, the ache in her core crested and in a moment of bliss she came apart again. She clung tightly onto him until the last shudder had passed and she was left breathless in his arms.

Miles nuzzled into Doria's neck before finally withdrawing from her and helping her back down onto the floor again. He brushed some stray strands of hair away from Doria's face before pressing a tender kiss upon her lips.

They stood against each other for a long moment, chests heaving. Miles stroked her cheek tenderly. "I knew you'd be magnificent."

Doria huffed a laugh, still dazed from their lovemaking. "Next time, a bed might be better."

"Next time?" Miles raised an eyebrow, a smile tugging at his lips. "Planning ahead, are we?"

Doria grinned, warmth flooding her at the implication. "Maybe I am."

The room lay still, cocooned in the soft afterglow of their shared passion. Doria's stormy eyes gazed at Miles with a mixture of tenderness and determination as she traced her fingers along the contours of his chest as they cuddled up on the reading sofa.

They hadn't talked about the curse, but Doria knew they needed to.

She told him about finding his photo in the library book and the discussion she'd had with Elenor and Cassondra.

"Whatever has bound you to this bookstore, Miles, we will find a way to free you," she said softly, her voice tinged with resolve.

Miles sighed, his blue eyes clouded with uncertainty. "Doria, the problem is that I don't know exactly how or why I was cursed. All I know is that Peter Smith was somehow involved."

Peter Smith was involved. She shouldn't be surprised. He always seemed to be skulking about.

Miles turned his head away, staring off into the dimly lit space of the quiet bookstore. "We had argued one day about business, and later that night, the shop was engulfed in flames. I found myself trapped inside, unable to leave. For those on the outside, the fire appeared to consume the shop and me along with it. But for me, it was a flash or flame and a moment of panic, then gone. When I tried to leave, the store wouldn't let me go. It's been like this ever since, never aging, always here." He shook his head, frustration creasing his brow. "I know Elenor and Cassie suspect you may be the key to breaking this curse, but I'm not sure how."

Doria's heart ached at the pain in his voice, and she felt a fierce protectiveness surge through her petite frame. Her rough past had taught her to be cautious, always vigilant, but something about Miles' gentle spirit had managed to pierce through her guarded exterior. The deep love they both held for books and stories served as a common thread that connected them, but somehow, over the past few days, the connection had grown so much stronger than a love of good fiction.

"Peter Smith...is there any other information about him? I mean, he hasn't seemed to age at all either. He looks to be the same age as me. Anything that could lead us to understand this curse?" She asked, searching Miles' face for any sign of hope. The snippet she'd read in the library hadn't mentioned the name of the arsonist who'd set Vespertine Books ablaze. Neither had Cassie or Elenor.

"Smith owned this bookstore before me," Miles offered, his voice barely a whisper. "Even after he'd signed the papers and I'd taken over, he kept popping in, telling me how I should be doing things. At first, I tried to be friendly about it, but then it just got to be too much. I asked him to leave one afternoon and he took offense. He was an odd man, interested in the darker aspects of the arcane. We disagreed on many things, especially the direction of the shop."

Doria's fingers tightened on his chest, and her thoughts raced. She knew that in order to break this curse, she would need to delve into a world she had never before encountered. But for Miles, she was willing to face whatever challenges lay ahead.

She traced her fingers over the elegant black script running up his arm.

"It's been here since the night I was bound. I'd burn it from my flesh if it meant my release."

"I've never seen writing like that before. What does it say?"

"No idea."

"Can I take a picture?" Doria was already reaching for her phone. "It's a place to start. Maybe I can find some way to get it translated."

"Be my guest."

She snapped a few, getting every angle and inch of his beautiful skin.

"Trust me, Miles," she whispered, eyes locked with his, full of determination. "I will find a way to set you free. And then you have to read all the books I suggest. Without complaint."

He yanked her off her feet and into his lap, then smiled against her mouth.

As their lips met once more, the room seemed to hum with energy, the shadows cast by the flickering candlelight.

"Promise me you'll be careful," Miles implored, his voice carrying a hint of vulnerability that betrayed the weight of his decades-long curse. His hands, strong yet tender, held Doria's petite frame with an almost desperate intensity. "I can't be out there with you. That's hard for me."

"Of course," Doria replied, her lips curving into a determined smile. "But I can't promise I won't do everything in my power to save you. I am a tough cookie, remember?" Her wavy dark hair framed her face, the shadows accentuating her fierce beauty.

He rested his forehead against hers.

"Power, trust, betrayal...these are the forces that have shaped our fates," Doria murmured, her fingers tracing the contours of Miles' face.

"And stories," he murmured.

"And stories," she agreed.

Without stories, she never would have been here. Without the love of a good book, she would have passed the worn sign without a second glance, magical or otherwise.

Without stories, she wouldn't have agreed to read a simple book and return to discuss it with the hunky nerd.

Without stories, she never would have believed any of this could be real.

As she stood to leave, the air around them seemed to hum with anticipation, as if the very walls of the bookstore bore witness to their unbreakable bond. Doria looked back at Miles, her gaze steady and unwavering.

"Until tomorrow," she whispered,

The weight of their impending parting hung heavy in the air, suffocating the room with an unspoken sorrow. Miles pulled Doria closer, his hands trembling as they cupped her face, and pressed a lingering kiss upon her lips – a desperate plea to remember him, should they never meet again. Her stormy eyes glistened with tears, yet she offered him a reassuring smile that tugged at the corners of her mouth.

"Remember," Doria whispered against his lips. "I will be back each day until we break this curse. You are not alone in this fight anymore."

Miles' pain was etched on his features at her words. They stood entwined, lost in the moment, as the shadows danced around them; the candlelight casting a warm glow upon their faces.

Doria nodded, her resolve unwavering. With a final glance filled with longing, she turned away from him and approached the door.

The ancient oak groaned under the weight of her touch, the worn brass handle cold against her palm. As she pushed it open, a gust of wind snatched at her dark, wavy hair, sending a shiver down her spine. She hesitated for only a moment, glancing back at Miles one last time before stepping out into the unknown.

The door slammed shut behind her, the sudden noise reverberating through the bookstore like a gunshot. Miles' heart constricted painfully in his chest as he watched the door's lock slide into place with a final, resounding click. The walls of the bookstore seemed to close in on him, the very air thick with the absence of Doria's presence.

He blinked back the tears threatening to spill over and whispered her name as if saying it aloud would bring her back to him. But she was gone, vanished into the night like a wraith, and he was left to face the emptiness that now consumed him.

"Power, trust, betrayal..." he murmured, echoing Doria's words from earlier. These were the forces that had shaped their fates, but they refused to be defined by them. And so, with a heavy heart, Miles awaited the return of the woman he knew he had fallen in love with, even if she didn't know it yet.

He had waited so long for her to arrive. He could wait a little bit more.

157

Interested in more of Doria and Miles? Their story continues in Vespertine Dreams, coming December of 2023.

## ABOUT THE AUTHOR

Aster Rye is a pen name of author Kami King Larsen. She grew up with a love for reading remarkable stories and cut her teeth on horror and sci-fi. While she still loves a good spine tingler, eventually she discovered the endless joy of fantasy and romance.

## More from Aster Rye

Writing as Kami King Larsen

*A Simple Tale of Water and Weeping*

*Blood and Wonder* (Medicus Corpus book 1)

*Breath and Starshine* (Medicus Corpus book2)

## Let's Connect

Join my mailing list for ARC books and other exciting news

www.kamikinglarsenbooks.com

Follow me on Instagram @authorkamikinglarsen

Or find me on Facebook Kami King Larsen Books and Bits